THE LOST

**Written by
Joe R. Moya**

Eliezer Tristan Publishing
Portland, OR

Cover design by Aaron Smith

**"Listen to them, the children of the night.
What beautiful music they make."**
Bela Lugosi, DRACULA

"The freaks come out at night."
Whoudini

"Look what your God has done to me!"
Gary Oldman, BRAM STOKER'S DRACULA

BLOODLETTING

It's funny. I was never afraid of the dark.

Lying on a deserted street corner in uptown Manhattan during the middle of the night, his body dying, and his throat ripped open, George Morelli pondered these last words that came to his mind.

My blood feels so warm...I can feel it gushing out my neck...oh God, I'm gonna die...why does it hurt so much? Why is this taking so long? Mom...help me Ma...please...Make it go away...

***

It was a little after midnight when George Morelli walked off the campus of Columbia University, located in the uppermost tip of Manhattan. He had just left the dorm room of Kaitlin Anderson, a nineteen-year-old freshman, very smart girl, and someone George had his eye on from the get go.

After weeks of sweet talk and gushing about her intellect, she finally invited him to her dorm room. After some small talk, they shared a joint laced with heroin from George's personal stash. He knew it was laced; she didn't. Being a small-time drug dealer had its perks.

A few nickel bags sold here and there were enough to get George a new wardrobe and some petty spending cash, but not enough to get his own place. George's mom would sometimes ask where he got his money from, and he'd lie and say he did computer repair work on the side. Not a bad deal for little mama's boy. No rent, free food and the use of his mother's new car. However, his living arrangement certainly put a crimp in his ability to score with chicks. They wanted guys who had their own place.

That's when George hit on the idea of messing with his fellow female college students who lived on campus. They already had their own spot, and they were more than willing to put that convenience to use. Instead of having to invite Kaitlin over to his parent's house, all George had to do was wait until her roommate went back home for Christmas break. All it took was that one joint for Kaitlin to get naked.

George was having a good time until Kaitlin wanted him to stop, right in the middle of intercourse. *Stop? Bitch, I'll stop when I bust a nut.* Ignoring her pleas, George kept plowing away, even after Kaitlin started crying and begging him to just stop.

Finally, George was finished. He laid on her bed catching his breath, while she got up and stumbled to the bathroom, still sobbing. George got up and got dressed, with the sounds of Kaitlin vomiting loudly in the background. He didn't bother to check on her or even tell her good-bye; he had a date to visit Angie Bello, the cute girl he met in his physics class. She told George to come by her apartment that night. Her parents were gone for the week (like Kaitlin's roommate, also on vacation), and George damn sure wasn't going to miss out on this opportunity. So, he left Kaitlin, still crying in the bathroom, and calmly walked out the door without saying a word to her.

Stepping outside in the cold winter air, he placed a call to Miss Bello letting her know he was on his way. George walked across the 231th Street Bridge on his way to Angie's apartment, thinking of how many ways he could get her to say "big dick" in Spanish-

Someone was walking behind him.

The sound was unmistakable. George quickly turned to see who it was, his hand on the .9 mm pistol in his jacket just in case someone tried to jack him, but there was no one there.

George stood for a minute, looking around for someone and listening for any other noise. There was snow on the ground, covering parked cars and fire hydrants, but that was it. There was nothing else. He was alone on the bridge, his heavy breathing the only sound to be heard.

I could've sworn I heard footsteps behind me, George thought. *Shit, it had to be that joint. I forget just how strong my stash is. That's why I'm the dope man.* Letting out a sigh of relief, George turned around and continued his walk across the bridge, laughing at his fear of that strange noise he thought he heard. He used to hear all kinds of things back when he was a kid in Hempstead, walking around at night-

Someone was walking behind him again.

He knew now that his mind was not playing tricks on him. The sound of footsteps was too close, too real…and it wouldn't go away.

George grabbed the gun from his jacket, turned around, and without a second thought, fired off several shots. He couldn't quite make out what he saw, except that he was firing into someone standing there. *Whoever that was is a dead motherfucker now*, he thought.

Ironically, George Morelli had no idea just how right he was.

It took a few seconds for George to notice two things: first, the person he shot was male, about six feet tall with a medium build. Second, this person was still standing…looking quite alive and unharmed.

Although many things were going through George's mind (*how the FUCK is this guy still standing, and where did he come from...*) he did not panic. He was a tough guy, used to hanging with the local *mafiosos* in his neighborhood, so he wasn't about to be scared off by a psycho in a black trench coat. George just assumed (*prayed*) he had missed. He quickly raised his gun, aimed it at the guy in the trench coat and fired off five more rounds, hitting his target square in the torso. There was no doubt George had connected this time.

Alas, there was also no doubt he had connected the first time, because the result was again the same…the guy in the trench coat standing his ground, looking quite well for someone who had just been shot multiple times.

The panic was swelling in George Morelli's bosom, rising like a tidal wave and threatening to overwhelm him…*Holy shit, oh my God my God what the fuck is GOING ON…*when suddenly the stranger started to walk toward him.

George had to force himself not to scream. Despite sensing a fear he had never encountered before in his life, he was determined not to let himself fall apart. There was a huge wad of cash in George's pockets. So, what if it belonged to Derrick from Brooklyn? Fuck him! He'd get his money back somehow. George's priority was to get out of here, to get away from the nightmare that was coming closer to him.

"Look man, I…I'm sorry about shooting you, OK? I got some money…look, here it is! See? It's all yours-"

It happened so fast.
The stranger raised his right hand…
…took a mighty swing…
…and ripped out the front half of George Morelli's throat.

Blood and skin tissue flew everywhere. George felt a shock of searing pain, a blast of frigid air where his throat used to be, and he could almost see where his larynx landed when it hit the ground. He tried to scream, but all that came out was a sick hissing sound mixed with drops of blood and spittle. Mercifully for George, his body went into shock and his mind into a state of shutting down.

The last few moments of George Morelli's life were a blur to him. All he could feel was the numbing pain of his injury and the wistful longings for his childhood, when he wasn't afraid of the dark and Mommy was there to make sure everything would be all right. *The pain is too much...Ma...make it stop, please...I can't take it anymore...let it be over...*

A strange sense of peace came over George, the knowledge that death was upon him. No more pain or fear. George would have died peacefully this way if he had been left alone, but that was not to be. The very last feeling he ever felt were two sharp fangs violently clamping down on his gaping wound.

VICKI

The cell phone started ringing, but Vicki Ramos couldn't hear it. She was too busy relaxing in her bathtub, enjoying a most satisfying bubble bath. Usually Vicki would bring the phone into the bathroom with her, just so she wouldn't miss a call. But this time was a little different.

Maybe she meant to bring it with her and just forgot; maybe she couldn't remember that she left it lying on the loveseat in her living room. Or maybe, at this particular moment, Vicki just wanted to leave it out there, so she could have a little bit of time to herself. The rays of early morning sunlight shone through the bathroom window, illuminating the bathroom in an almost surrealistic glow. Vicki noticed how the sunlight gleamed on the bath bubbles. Pretty nice, she thought to herself. Pretty incredible too, that she even had time to reflect on such a sight, not to mention time for a bubble bath. But Vicki was not complaining. Even a dedicated career woman like her had to take a break *sometime*.

Victoria Elizabeth Ramos, Vicki to everyone but her parents, was not the type of woman to take much of a break from anything. She had seen a lot of things growing up as a child in the Bronx, sitting by the living room window of her family's sixth-floor apartment. Vicki wanted to do her observing from the fire escape, but her mother was afraid she'd fall off or something. When Vicki wasn't busy catching a glimpse of Yankee Stadium or counting the cars that drove by on Edward L. Grant Highway, she would sometimes look down and observe the people on the street. This always interested her, mainly because she got to see something new happen every day. The smelly guy who lived on the first floor making his daily trip to the local liquor store. The elderly couple from the house across the street taking a rare stroll outside. Mrs. Brown, the nice lady who lived next door, making her daily tip to the bus stop.

But the one thing Vicki saw that truly disturbed her was the sight of her father coming home from his construction job. Not because she wasn't happy to see him. On the contrary, the daily highlight of Vicki's childhood was usually her *papi* walking in the door and giving her a big hug. It was when he sat down gingerly on the sofa, the pain etched on his face as he bent over to untie his work boots, that Vicki would feel uncomfortable, sometimes looking away to the side. Her father was a young man, a strong man, but every night on that sofa, all Vicki could see was someone who looked old and tired…a man whose spirit was willing but whose body most often was not. She couldn't understand why this had to happen, or why her mother would sometimes cry in her bedroom, worrying how the rent was going to be paid that month, or why her family could work so hard and yet be so poor.

Vicki was always the determined one in the family, the little *nena* who was sweet and respectful but hard headed and steadfast. "Sugar on the outside and fire on the inside," was how her grandfather described her. When Vicki made up her mind, there was no changing it back. The door was shut, discussion finished, case closed. Seeing her beloved father moaning in pain just to take off his shoes, little Vicki Ramos decided that she was going to do things differently.

Vicki got up out of her bathtub, stepping on the white T-shirt she threw on the floor. She had meant to get a bath rug, but then decided that a dirty piece of clothing about to be thrown in the hamper served the purpose just fine. As long as there was some kind of soft material keeping her pampered feet from touching the wood floor, she was happy. The fact that she had to drag the shirt under her feet from the bathroom to the bedroom was a minor inconvenience…until today. Right before Vicki got a chance to place her clean toes on the rug in her room, her phone started ringing again, meaning she would have to drag the shirt under her feet from the bedroom to the living room and back. MAJOR inconvenience.

"Perfect timing," Vicki grumbled to herself. She dragged her T-shirt covered feet across the hallway as fast as she could, mindful of the fact that her blinds were open and that she didn't bother to completely cover herself before she went to get the phone. *Just my luck that some pervert would look through the window right about now*, she thought, *Bueno, if that doesn't give him the thrill of his life, then I better take my ass back to the gym.*

If some lucky old gent *had* seen Vicki naked in her window, he would have indeed gotten the thrill of his life. She stood five feet six inches tall, with long black, wavy hair, baby brown eyes and the type of face that would always look young. Alas, no man was that lucky today. As Vicki grabbed her phone, she saw a familiar number displayed, and let out a small sigh.

"Hey Nathan."

"Ramos! Hey, where are you? I've been calling for half an hour already."

"Sorry about that. I was in the shower and left my phone out in the living room." *Running half-naked across my apartment just to talk to my boss. Do I love my job or what?*

"I'm on a deadline, Vick. I don't have time for your personal hygiene." Vicki hated that nickname, but never said anything about it. Nathan was a good supervisor who always looked out for her, and she knew that was a rare thing in this business. Putting up with a stupid nickname was a very small price to pay. "I got something for you."

Nathan Tibbs was the station manager at WABC-TV, where Vicki Ramos was a rising star. In just three years, she'd gone from an intern to community reports to the station's number one live scene reporter. She always seemed to be at the right place at the right time, at times getting live scoops before other stations even knew what was going on. Vicki had been offered the 6 o'clock co-anchor position, and she was getting preliminary offers from several networks as well, but Vicki loved the action of being a street reporter. She knew that anchoring from a desk wouldn't provide the same kind of rush she got from reporting from the scene of a live incident.

Naturally, there was a lot of resentment and jealousy at WABC towards Vicki's quick success. Some people felt that she was being pushed because she was a young Hispanic female, and that the station was using her to appeal to that demographic for higher ratings. Others thought that she was either the daughter of a drug dealer or was dating one. Still others believed that Vicki got it done the old-fashioned way…by sleeping with everyone from the CEO to the night shift maintenance man. After all, it worked for so many others.

But in Vicki's case, it was a combination of hard work and knowing the right people. Not people in upper management but on the streets…her family and friends in the Bronx. Vicki had built up a network of friends, family and paid associates who were almost always in the know about certain events in the city. They were more than happy to tip her off to anything that was going down or was about to go down. Vicki never walked around acting like she was better than anybody else, just because she had money and lived nice and was something of a local celebrity. She knew where she came from and never was ashamed of it, and the people in her old neighborhood loved her for that.

It didn't hurt that Vicki worked harder than anybody else did at the station, a fact that did not go unnoticed by management. She had made a lot of sacrifices in her life the last three years, but it was well worth it. At 26, Vicki Ramos was the hottest news personality in The Big Apple…

"Whatever you got for me better be good, Nathan. I'm standing half-naked in my living room dripping water on the floor."

"Thanks for the visual, Vick. It's a good one all right, story wise at least. Damn sure isn't good for the poor guy involved. There's been a murder in upper Manhattan on the 231st Street Bridge."

"Oh. OK," Vicki replied. Despite reporting on it all the time in her line of work, she never got used to the news of someone being murdered. One would think that Vicki wouldn't be fazed by death, being a native New Yorker and growing up in the area that she did. But there is a big difference between someone dying from an accident or a drug overdose and someone else laid out on a street corner in a pool of their own blood. It was the cold-bloodedness of such an act that bothered Vicki, the total disregard for the life of another human being. She knew that reporting on murders was a part of the job, and she so far had managed to keep her personal feelings apart from her work. Still, it was not an easy thing for her to deal with.

"What's the M.O.? Shot, stabbed, run over…?"

"Er…not quite." Nathan paused for a second before his next sentence. "From what we've been told, a young white male was found on the bridge with his throat ripped out."

"Oh my God!" Vicki said, her face contorted into a look of disgust. "Are you serious, Nate? This sounds bad. I don't think we'll be able to shoot anywhere near the scene now. There's probably blood splashed all over the snow, and you know the higher ups won't let us put that on the air."

Nathan paused slightly before speaking. "Actually, Vick, that won't be a problem. There isn't any blood on the scene at all."

REASONS

Vicki Ramos leaned against her Chrysler 300, pulled alongside the curb of the road at the Manhattan entrance of the 231th Street Bridge. She hated being outside in thirty-two degree weather (times like this she wondered why she didn't take that offer from WTVJ in Miami), but she wanted to get a clear view of the scene on the bridge. The police had already taped off a section of the southbound lane, right by the sidewalk. Although Vicki stood only about fifty feet away, she couldn't make out anything else due to the large amount of police blocking her view. *There's more cops out there than usual for a murder*, Vicki thought. *I wish Louis would hurry up and get here.*

Besides wanting a better view of the action, Vicki was also a bit too nervous to wait inside her car. The remark Nathan made about no blood found at the scene weirded her out. All she could think of while driving to the bridge was how little sense it made to her. A guy's throat is ripped out and there's no blood? That's just not possible. Vicki told Nathan that he either got the wrong information or someone was playing a sick joke on him.

"Don't bet on it," Nathan told her. "My friend at the prescient gets this stuff straight from the police dispatch, so it's no joke."

Those words hung in Vicki's mind as she stood at the entrance of the bridge. Sure, New York City was full of weirdos, but this was a little too extreme, not to mention impossible.

Vicki's thought pattern was interrupted when she noticed a news van parked much closer to the action than she was. Standing just a few feet from the van, right at the foot of the crime scene, was Anna Jennings, reporter for Channel 4 News. Dressed to the nines, talking to the camera with just a hint of a smirk, conducting a live report. It's at that precise moment when Vicki realized she'd just been scooped.

Can you believe this shit? Jennings is here before I am! I can't believe SHE of all people got here before me. Dammit. None of my sources tipped me off about this…and I know people around here, too! I KNOW Jennings doesn't have any good sources. She usually gets her tips from ME. She must've got a hell of a lucky break to scoop me on this one. The van isn't even here yet! Where the hell is Louis?

Almost as if on cue, a WABC-TV news van appeared on the scene, parking behind Vicki's car. Opening the driver's side door was a tall, heavyset man in his mid-forties named Louis Tennio, Vicki's cameraman. Louis is the guy who tagged along with Vicki on her reports, getting some great shots along the way. It took him a while to get used to her style of reporting, which almost always consisted of starting her report before they even got to the scene. It was a shock at first, but Louis learned to love it. He, too, fell in love with the rush of a live event, the feeling that he never knew what was gonna happen next but he was damn sure going to catch it on film.

But Louis wasn't the one getting tips or cultivating sources. He was just the cameraman. It was up to Vicki to give the green light on when and where something was going on, and to give Louis enough time to gather all his gear. This morning she called him at 7:49 a.m. and told him to meet her at the 231th Street Bridge in upper Manhattan, right near his apartment building…and oh, by the way, she was about 10 minutes from there so he needed to hurry up.

"Ten minutes? What are you, crazy?" Louis responded,

but Vicki had already hung up. So being the true professional, Louis threw on a sweat suit and his leather jacket, grabbed his camera equipment and ran out the door. *She better not make any smart-ass remarks about my morning breath*, he thought.

Moments later, Vicki and Louis were setting up for a live report on the bridge. They had gotten near the crime scene, but not as close as the Channel 4 team had gotten. Jennings and her crew were about ten feet from the body. Their cameraman had a great shot of the victim's feet, covered with the customary yellow blanket. Vicki and Louis had to set up on the other side of the bridge, a good thirty feet away. From Vicki's vantage point, all that Louis could capture was a glimpse of the blanket sticking out from behind a horde of policeman. The NYPD's general rule of thumb when dealing with the press at a live scene is basically first come, first serve. If you arrive soon enough to set up a good shot, fine. If not, you get stuck with whatever crumbs they throw your way. Usually, Vicki Ramos would be the one who got there first. Not today.

"Can you believe this, Louie?" Vicki complained. "Anna Jennings gets first dibs on this story before I do. This is ridiculous!"

"She must've hit the tipster lottery this morning" Louis replied. "Even a blind squirrel finds a nut once in a while. Shit happens."

"Yeah but this shit is happening on my turf."

"So, what happened to your sources? Somebody around here must've heard this guy scream."

"I have no clue, Louie. But I will find out. Somebody's gonna hear me bitch today, and it's not gonna be pretty. And what's the deal with your breath? Haven't you heard of Scope?"

Louis shot Vicki a look of slight contempt. "Haven't you heard of giving your cameraman enough time to USE Scope?"

Vicki was about to reply with a comeback when she recognized one of the officers at the scene, Terrance

Whitmore. A member of her high school graduating class, real nice guy, who just so happened to be one of her secret sources. *I might get lucky this morning, after all.* "Wait here, Louis," Vicki says, "I'll be back with some info in a minute." Turning her charm on to the max, Vicki walked over to Terrance.

"Hey stranger."

Terrance turned, slightly surprised. "Hey yourself. What happened to you? I figured you'd be the first media person here. As usual."

"It's a long story. Listen, I need some info quick. What's the 411?"

Terrance looked around, making sure no one was within earshot, and then spoke to Vicki in a hushed tone. "This is freaky, Vicki. I swear, I've never seen anything like this since I've been a cop, and I've seen a lot. This shit is just blowing everyone's mind."

A chill ran through Vicki's body, the same weird feeling she felt when talking to Nathan. "I heard that there was no blood at the scene. Is that true?"

"Only a few drops here and there. Thing is, the guy's throat was just ripped out, totally. I mean, it looks like he was attacked by a shark. But check this out. First, there's hardly any blood around the body. All we found was some small drops in the snow and on his jacket. That's it. There should have been a pool of blood all over the snow, but there wasn't anything. Then, we can't find the rest of his throat. No skin pieces, no tissue, nothing. The forensic guys are still looking around in the snow. They think the skin fragments might have been frozen over or something. Plus the guy wasn't robbed. He was carrying about $500 in cash and some nickel bags of heroin on him. But that's not the weirdest thing."

Jesus, if THAT'S not the weirdest thing, I don't think I wanna hear it, Vicki thought.

"The weirdest thing," said Terrance, "is that the guy was shooting at someone, most likely his assailant. We found a .9 mm with an empty clip and a bunch of casings on the ground, and a set of footprints leading to and away from the body. This fucking guy emptied out seventeen rounds at someone and still got ripped open. Either he's a piss poor shot or…I don't know. Like I told you, Vicki, this is some freaky shit. Some Rick James, super freak type of shit."

"No doubt," Vicki said.

The nervous feeling she'd had since she first spoke with Nathan was now starting to nestle permanently inside her bosom. No matter how hard she tried, she was not able to shake the feeling that something just wasn't right about this, besides the obvious. She had the sense that Terrance had the same feelings too, although he would never admit it.

"Listen, thanks for the info, sweetie. I've got to get working on my report." Vicki gave Terrance a quick kiss on the cheek then turned to leave. "Lunch is on me next time I see you. Please be careful, OK?"

Terrance smiled, patting the gun in his holster. "Don't worry, mamacita. I plan on it."

Vicki watched her high school friend walk back towards the crime scene. *I hope you don't end up having to rely on that thing, sweetie,* she thought. *After hearing what you just told me, I doubt it would make a damn bit of difference.*

PRAYER

Vicki Ramos lay on her bed and stared at the clock on her nightstand. 10:47 stared back at her in bright, red numbers. At this time of night, she would usually be doing one of three things; prepping for a live report, wrapping up a report she had just done, or getting some needed sleep. And if there was ever a day that deserved to end in slumber for Miss Ramos, it was today. She caught grief from Nathan about getting beat to the punch by Channel 4, then had to listen to Louis complain about the short notice in the morning, followed by staying at the station and going over her report a million times so that it would look like she *had* been the first reporter at the scene, a decision handed down from upper management so as not to "disappoint" her viewers. Sleep was calling her. But tired as she was, Vicki was far from getting any kind of sleep.

The death of George Morelli had been on her mind all day. The bad feeling she felt in the morning after speaking with Nathan had not gone away. It gnawed at her constantly, slowly eating away at any sense of security she had, and now it was preventing her from falling asleep. Vicki felt a strong sense that there was something more to this crime than what was on the surface. What that "something" was she couldn't put her finger on. The official police line was that Morelli had died from "blunt trauma to the throat, nearly resulting in decapitation." They would not confirm the reports by Vicki (and that bitch from Channel 4) stating there was no blood found at the scene.

It went deeper than that for Vicki, though. This went beyond just having a "creepy" feeling about a murder. This was something that troubled her very soul. Vicki did what any other rational adult would do when faced with a sense of fear so disturbing, it made sleep and peace of mind impossible: she called her mother.

"Hello?"

"Mami? It's Vicki."

"Victoria! *Que pasa, mi nina*? Why are you up so late? You're usually out doing a report or falling asleep by now."

"I know. It's nothing, just… not feeling too good. I had a hectic day at work. Did you see the report I did for the six o'clock show?"

"No, baby, I missed it. Your father's appointment with Dr. Tapia ran late. His back is getting better, you know. He's sleeping now."

"*Para siempre*. I'll talk to him tomorrow. Don't worry about the report. I'll let you see it sometime this week. Not my best work, but it's OK."

"What's wrong, *mi amor*? You don't sound too good. What's wrong?"

"Mami, will you do me a small favor?"

"What is it? Tell me."

"When you pray tonight, ask the Lord to help me relax and sleep tonight, and to clear my mind of stress and… other things. I did a report on a murder today and it's just been… really bothering me all day."

"*Si, mi amor*, I'll do that. I was getting ready to pray when you called. Was the murder that bad, Victoria?"

"Yeah, mami, it was. I'll tell you about it later. I'm sorry, I'm just so tired right now…"

"It's ok, try to get some rest. I'll pray for you tonight, because you need your sleep. Call me tomorrow and let me know if you feel better."

"I will. I'm going to sleep now. Thank you, mami. Give daddy and everyone else a kiss for me."

"Good night, Victoria. I love you."

"I love you too, mami. Good night."

MARCUS

The hunger is approaching.

Perched on a rooftop overlooking Upper Manhattan, stood a vampire named Marcus. Standing 6 feet tall, with a slim yet muscular frame, easily passing for a twenty something white male. Marcus looked every bit a living breathing human. But behind the handsome packaging was a creature of the night. An undead bloodsucker. Yet unlike most vampires, this particular one was not hunting, but reflecting.

The sight from this rooftop is incredible. There were never cities like this back home. The city skyline illuminates the night. I'd love to see the city during the daylight hours, but I'm not human anymore. That was taken from me 200 years ago. Every moment I spend walking this earth, I curse what's been done to me. Forced to drink the blood of the living.
I'm starting to doubt the reason for doing this. Coming to America, leaving the underground clan we've called home for centuries to make our own.... is it worth it all? The others must be wondering the same thing. Each day, they grow more restless. Each day, their hunger grows. How much longer before innocent blood is no longer forbidden? If that happens, everything we've worked for and all that we've hoped would happen, would be lost forever.
We left Sarajevo with a common purpose, a goal which

may be too late to achieve. But we can't give up. Those who followed Jesus Christ told endless tales of his love for all, even for those who sin. What about those whose very existence is based upon committing acts of sin? What about the dead wishing to undo what's already been done? Are we beyond salvation? Should I even attempt to speak to the Son of God? Would Lucifer destroy me for even thinking that?

No. If he had the power to do so, we'd all be wiped out. We've had these thoughts for many years. Our so-called Dark Father is nothing. His only power is over those who follow him, and they're the ones we must worry about.

For a long time, the vampire stood on the roof. How long was anyone's guess. Hours? Minutes? The answer was unknown, but it was enough time for the hunger within Marcus to bubble up to the surface. The bloodsucker had done pretty well keeping the hunger in check, but it would not last forever, and now the inner beast was demanding to be fed.

Uhhh...the hunger...I can't hold it back anymore. It wants to feed. I MUST feed. Yesterday, the blood of that human in the alley was enough, but just barely. His blood was just like everyone else in this city... thin and weak, with an unclean taste. Licking his blood off the walls made me sick. Some things even a vampire can't stomach. That piece of glass he used on me is still lodged in my leg...

Marcus saw her. A woman on the sidewalk, carrying bags and walking alone. No one else on the street except her. The smell of her blood hit Marcus like a sledgehammer. He could almost taste her sweet, sweet blood on his dead lips.

...uuhhhh...the time has come...I must feed. There she is...a human female. Young and vibrant. Thick, rich blood flows through her...NO!! I can't kill her. She's an innocent.

Every step the female human took brought her closer

to where Marcus was. It would be easy for him to reach her from here. Just a few seconds really. That close to the sweet relief his undead body craved.

Except Marcus knew the cost of that relief. A cost his inner self was not willing to give; a price his bloodlust was all too willing to pay.

She must be spared...
but I can't hold back...must have her blood...
NO! She's an innocent, she must be spared...
she must be eaten...

The vampire leapt off the rooftop, focused on the young woman below on the street. Within seconds, he would be upon her. Within seconds, he would finally quench the raging desire in his bosom

must have her blood, must have HER, HER BLOOD,
SO THICK AND...HAVE HER, MUST FEED BLOOD FEED
MUST I MUST HAVE BLOOD HER BLOOD ANY BLOOD I
MUST....

***

Denise Crawford heard a whoosh of air behind her. The night had already been windy enough as it was. This was different. This wind blew directly behind her. She quickly turned to see what it could be. But there was nothing there. She was all alone on this Manhattan sidewalk. Denise normally didn't like to go out this time of night, but it was a beautiful winter night, and she just couldn't resist. Now however she was feeling nervous, as if there was something there she couldn't see. She knew she heard a loud whoosh of wind behind her, there was no question. Maybe it was a small gust? A micro-burst, as they say. Whatever it was, the phenomenon was gone.

Mrs. Crawford was a smart girl. She wasn't about to

linger around and try to figure out what the strange wind was. Denise walked at a brisk pace the rest of the way to her apartment, making a mental note to never again let a nice winter evening coax her into shopping out at night.

BLOODLUST

Vicki Ramos lay on her bed, emerged in a deep sleep. It seemed her mother's prayer had worked. Not long after hanging up with her mother, Vicki fell asleep. The bright, red numbers on her clock read 6:04. The earliest rays of sunlight were creeping though her window blinds. The clock read 6:05 when the phone began to ring. It wasn't until the fifth ring that Vicki woke up, clutching the phone and answering in a gravelly voice

".....Hello..."

"Wake up, Boricua. It's Alex. I got a scoop for ya."

"...uhhhh....wh-what's up?"

"How fast can you get down to Amsterdam?"

46 minutes later... WABC-TV's morning program... anchor Alixa Castellanos.

"We take you now to Vicki Ramos reporting live from the New York Blood Center on Amsterdam Avenue in Manhattan.

Vicki, how are things over there?"

"Alixa, behind me, you'll see that police have closed off the area leading into the Blood Center. From here, you can see that the front doors leading into the center have been torn off. What we know so far is that one or more intruders broke into the Center approximately sometime between midnight and 6 a.m. There is some damage done inside and it appears that several containers of blood are missing, although police are not saying exactly how much.

With me right now is Blood Center coordinator Robert Tucker, who was the first center employee to see the damage. Mr. Tucker, can you tell us how bad the damage is inside?"

"Uh, there is a significant amount of damage inside the center. We have glass all over the floor, there are tables and chairs knocked over, and the doors to the freezer were...it looks like they were forcibly removed."

"Any idea how the doors might have been taken off?"

"I can't answer that question right now. Or any question regarding how much, if any, blood might be missing."

"Have the police told you anything about a possible motive for this attack?"

"Again, I can't answer that question. All I can say is that it's a mess in there."

"Thank you for time, Mr. Tucker. That's about all from here. As soon as police reveal more information, we'll have it for you. Back to you, Alixa."

***

At that same moment, underneath a building several blocks away, the vampire named Marcus kneeled on a dirty basement floor, surrounded by numerous empty blood bags. He greedily chugged blood from a bag, only stopping when every last drop was exhausted.

Better. Much better. The hunger is gone for now. I couldn't contain myself anymore. I thought I'd be able to control it until I found someone I could feed on. I almost killed that girl on the street. The intense hunger couldn't persuade me to drink her blood. I'm glad the blood bank was close by. It was my only option.

This blood from the bank is cold, and doesn't absorb into the body as well as fresh blood. But it's better than nothing. I feel like an animal... like the wild creatures that roam the forests of Europe. Damn you, Vladimir. You did this to me, to all of us. I curse the fucking ground you walk on.

This has got to stop. What we're searching for has to come soon. I don't know how much longer we can keep from killing innocents. Tonight was the closest I've come to killing one since we left home. I cannot…I WILL not…do anything to jeopardize our mission, but how much longer can any of us hold out?

I have to find an answer soon…

ALEXANDER

A young man named Carlos paced the floor of his bedroom talking on a phone, unaware that a vampire hidden in the shadows outside was watching him.

"What up, Richie? Listen up. Hey, are you alone? Go outside and talk. This is private."

Carlos waited for his friend to go outside, nervously pacing back and forth in his bedroom. The time was half past 11 p.m. He glanced at his girlfriend Millie lying in their bed, having finally cried herself to sleep. Carlos felt just a twinge of remorse for slapping her around a little while ago, but then quickly reminded himself that, as usual, she deserved it.

He told Millie to stop talking to the guy who worked at the store across the street, but she didn't listen. She kept babbling on with that "he's just a friend" bullshit. Carlos thought she would have learned something from the last time he beat her down, but obviously her memory was in need of some refreshing. When Millie came home earlier tonight, the first thing Carlos did was apologize in advance for what he was about to do, then proceeded to slap her face so hard her lip split open. A few more smacks, some hair pulling, and a good bashing of her head against the wall was enough to make Carlos think that maybe this time she would fucking listen.

This was not the right time for him to deal with any

bullshit from her. Carlos was helping to set up a huge cocaine transaction for the next night. His boss had entrusted him with making the contact with sellers from Philadelphia, as well as to when and where the buy was going to take place. Everything was in place and ready to go. Carlos was nervous but excited, and he didn't need any extra problems with his girl. He didn't even have time to put a bullet in the guy who Millie was talking to. Carlos figured the punk could live another day while the deal was being done. Tomorrow, he would take care of this little problem personally.

Meanwhile, the eyes of the undead watched him from outside the window.

"Richie, you ready? Check it out. It's gonna go down tomorrow night in Harlem, at the warehouse docks by 125th and the Hudson. Around this time, maybe a little later. Depends on how fast they can get here from Philly. They're bringing a shitload of blow in a ConEd truck. I'm telling you Richie, we're gonna be stacking papers, son. Serious fucking money. Shit'll sell like fuckin' crazy. So you got it? I'll get you around eleven tomorrow night. Boss is gonna ride with me. All right? I'm gone."

***

Sitting in the fire escape in front of the bedroom window, the vampire could see Carlos hang up the phone and turn off the light. This was to be the night Carlos met a violent death, but the information he relayed to his friend on the phone was enough to save his life…for now. Instead of one killing for one vampire, it would now be a smorgasbord for the entire group. They would have to wait 24 hours, but they'd been among the undead for centuries now, so one more day wouldn't make a difference.

The vampire decided it was time to leave. It jumped off the fire escape and effortlessly landed on the street six stories below, as if jumping off a milk carton. Looking around to make sure no one saw the jump, Alexander calmly walked away. Several blocks away, under the railroad tracks, Alexander was met by his longtime friend, Marcus.

"I didn't make the kill," Alexander explained.

"Was there an innocent close-by?" Marcus replied.

"Yeah, but that didn't have anything to do with it," said Alexander. *Not sure that it would've stopped me anyway. Once I get going, it's hard to stop.* "It's amazing what little things you can find out sitting next to a window."

"Now you got me curious. I can't wait to hear about it."

"But of course, Marcus. I love to share good news. Tell the others to get ready. There's gonna be a blood bath tomorrow night, and we're crashing the party."

INFORMATION

The smell of bacon and eggs filled the area of Vicki's kitchen. It was a beautiful sunny Friday morning, and Vicki was in the mood to cook. Her cameraman Louis sat at her kitchen table, enjoying the aroma of breakfast.

"You know what, Vicki? I might just get up and rush out the apartment a little earlier from now on. I'd be worth it."

"Nice try, Louis." Vicki brought two plates filled with bacon, eggs, toast, and *platanos* to the table, then sat down. "I usually don't cook breakfast. I'm too damn tired and busy. But I really appreciate you coming out super early the last two days. So this is my way of showing my appreciation. And you better like my cooking!"

Louis takes a bite of the bacon and egg sandwich on his plate. "You ain't got to worry about that, Vicki. This is some damn good food you got here. Your mom taught you well."

"Thank you. Getting up that early must be hell on your sex life, huh?"

"Vicki, I've been married 22 years. I don't have a sex life."

Vicki and Louis both broke out in laughter, a friendly exchange broken up by Vicki's phone ringing.

"Hold on, Louis. Let me get the phone. Hello? Millie! How you been, girl? Got any good stuff for me?"

Twenty minutes later, Vicki and Louis are riding in the

WABC news van down a Manhattan street.

"Thanks for giving me enough time to swallow the orange juice," says Louis, with just a hint of sarcasm.

"Sorry, but this is too big to wait for anything," replied Vicki, sitting in the passenger seat scribbling down notes. "We've gotta get down to the station right now and get all the stuff we'll need. This thing is gonna happen tonight. Can you believe this, Louie? A real-live big time drug deal, and we're gonna catch it on camera!"

"Who is this chick, anyway? How does she know about this thing?"

"Millie? She's an old friend of mine. Her boyfriend is the one who's setting it up. She's one of my sources, drops me some info here and there. I used to go to college with her. She was supposed to graduate in the same class as me, but she dropped out her second year. I think it was to be with this *sangano* she's with now."

"English, please, English! What's a *sangano*?"

"What's a *sangano*? Someone like you! Anyway, he did something last night to really piss her off. I don't know exactly what he did, she wouldn't tell me, but it was enough for her to really want to fuck him over. She doesn't want to go the police because she doesn't trust them, so instead she called me. Once we get this thing filmed and throw it on the air, her boyfriend is done. And he's on probation too, so that makes it even worse. He's gonna go away for a long time, thanks to her. Louie, just think what this will do for our careers."

Louis glances over at Vicki with a look of concern. "You do know that this is gonna be dangerous, right? That we're stepping into a situation no sane person would step into? And if they catch us, we're gonna die, Vicki."

Vicki paused for a second to contemplate the reality of the situation. If her parents knew what she was about to do, they'd tie her to the bed. What if they did get caught? Her family would be devastated. Louis had a wife and two kids. They would lose a father and a husband.

"I know. So let's not get caught!"

Vicki and Louis again broke out in laughter, an acknowledgment that this would be dangerous, but what the hell…they're crazy enough to try it.

Louis was caught up in the enthusiasm. "Hey, I'm as excited about this as you are. It's a cameraman's dream to catch something like this on film, especially as it's happening. But you know we won't be able to use our names on this thing. It'd be suicide."

"I know, but that's OK. The only ones who need to know are the people who sign our paychecks, and I guarantee you when they see what we've done, those paychecks are gonna get a lot bigger."

"You got that right," Louis replies, giving Vicki a high-five. Everything felt right for Vicki Ramos this morning. She had just gotten the biggest scoop of her career, one that would propel her salary through the roof. Vicki had totally forgotten about the weird feeling she felt two days earlier. The numbing fear that had threatened to rob her of sleep and peace of mind was all gone, replaced by the excitement of what lay ahead for her. *I have a good feeling about tonight. This will be the night that will change my life.*

Vicki could never imagine just how right she was.

CONFRONTATION

The ConEd truck filled with a shitload of cocaine pulled into the 125th Street docks behind a large warehouse. It was 12:08 a.m., very early Saturday morning, although for those heading out into the Manhattan nightlife, it was still Friday night. It wouldn't hit Saturday until the sun came up, longer if you had a hangover.

The individuals present at the docks were not worried about hangovers or partying or going to any clubs. They were there to make money. Following the truck into the docks were two Lincoln Continentals and a Hummer. They joined the three Ford Expeditions and the Cadillac El Dorado already parked there waiting for them. About 30 feet behind the Cadillac, Vicki and Louis sat hidden behind a large stack of crates. Both have been at the same spot for over an hour, talking to each other in hushed tones. Now the show was about to start, and they were both ready. Having already positioned his camera between two crates, Louis started to film. Vicki knelt right next to him, catching a glimpse of the action.

"All right, Vicki. This is it," whispered Louis. "We're filming. I wish we could've done a live feed of this thing."

"Me too," Vicki whispered back. "But it's too dangerous. Too many things involved that can screw the whole thing up. Doesn't matter, we're getting it now."

"I hope this thing doesn't take long," Louis muttered.

"I've only got 30 minutes of continuous tape in here."

"Trust me, it won't be that long," Vicki replied, very quietly. "They both want to get this done and get out of here as quickly as possible."

The Lincolns and the Hummer parked in front of the other cars. Four men emerge from each car. At the same time, several more men emerged from the Fords and the Cadillac. In all, there are 26 men involved in the transaction. Carlos, the woman beater, walked toward the other men with his boss, carrying a large briefcase. Two other men stepped forward towards Carlos, one of them carrying a manila envelope containing the registration and the keys to the truck.

Vicki bit her lip, barely able to contain her excitement. "There it is…the exchange. Oh my God, Louis, this is it," Vicki whispered, the excitement evident in her voice.

Louis stayed quiet, focusing all his attention on the task at hand. He zoomed in for a series of close shots. Carlos opening the briefcase…the man with the envelope and the truck keys looking at the stack of money inside the briefcase… counting the money to his satisfaction… both parties agreeing that it was a done deal... the clear shots of their faces... Louis caught it all on his camera. There wasn't anything going on at the docks that Louis had missed.

Except for the thick, foggy mist rolling along the ground.

Finally, the exchange between money and cocaine was complete. The money-filled briefcase switched places with the envelope and the truck keys. The deal done, both parties got ready to leave.

"That's it," Louis whispered. "Almost done. Lemme just get a few more faces in for good measure. Make sure all these pricks go down.

Vicki said nothing; she just smiled at the thought of what Louis and she were accomplishing. It was right about this time, when the dollar figures started floating around in her head, that she noticed how cold her legs were. Now granted it was 36 degrees outside, it was February, and Vicki was right by the river, but what got Vicki's attention was how it suddenly got even colder, real fast.

Damn, it got cold as hell all of a sudden. Feels like a draft. Vicki turned around just in time to see the thick mist creep along the ground, circling her legs, rising higher and higher. *What the hell is this???* So taken aback by what she was seeing, Vicki barely noticed the mist coming up behind Louis, creeping out further onto the dock…towards where the dealers were.

The fog rose higher, rising to almost eye level with Vicki. Then, like an old wound re-opening, the dreadful feeling she dealt with two days earlier suddenly returned with a vengeance.

I have a bad feeling about this.

Kneeling behind Louis, Vicki turned to say something to him when she looked off to the side and saw, directly in front of her, a pair of blood-red eyes… attached to a pale-skinned face… and a mouth with long, sharp fangs.

She stared directly into the face of a vampire.

It took about a good three seconds for the scream to travel from Vicki's gut to her mouth. What came out was not a silly scream, or something you would hear in the movies. No, what came out was the sound of a human being scared to the very fiber of their soul, the sound of someone who had looked into the face of the Devil himself and was screaming for the Lord to pull them away.

Carlos and the other dealers quickly turned around at the sound of the scream. His friend Richie, whom he had picked up earlier, yelled out loud, "What the fuck is that?!"

"That came from those crates," Carlos yelled back. "Somebody's there! It's a fucking set-up!" In a small corner in the back of his mind, Carlos wondered if Millie had anything to do with this.

The man who sold them the cocaine stared at the crates, then back at Carlos. "Fuck you man, we didn't set up shit! You're fucking 5-0!" The associates on both sides started to pull their weapons.

During all of this, Vicki was still screaming. The face was gone, but the mist remained. Louis, who almost dropped the camera in shock when the screaming started, frantically tried to quiet Vicki down, knowing in the back of his mind that because of her screaming they were both as good as dead. And it would appear he was right, as Carlos pulled out a Tech-9 from his jacket and aimed at the stack of crates. "Fuck you, pigs! That's your ass!"

No one noticed that the mist had now totally surrounded the entire dock, waist high to everyone. No one noticed the figures moving through the mist. No one…until right before Carlos pulled the trigger that would kill Louis and Vicki. A hand reached out in a lightning-quick motion and grabbed Carlos by the throat, pulling him down into the thick, white mist.

Bullets flew into the air, mixed with the sounds of Carlos screaming. His friend Richie yelled for him. "CARLOS!" In a moment of panic, Richie started shooting wildly into the area where Carlos was, spraying the entire area. The bullets did not hit Carlos (not that it would've mattered, as he was already quite dead), however the rounds did strike five members of both parties.

The docks quickly turned into a scene of chaos.

"Get the fuck outta here!!! Go!! Go!!!" yelled the man who sold the cocaine, as he ran to his car. He reached the door handle and had started to open the door. He never got inside. A heavy weight knocked him on his back… a heavy dead weight.

The man's face bruised from hitting the pavement, the drug dealer turned to look up and saw Alexander on top of him. "Hey, Mr. Pusherman. Thanks for the free food," said the vampire. Too late the dealer opened his mouth to scream, as Alexander slammed his fangs into the human's neck.

Vicki stopped screaming, slowly recovering from seeing something, and began to notice the sounds going on around her. Louis looked like death warmed over, but he was still pointing the camera towards where the drug dealers were moments ago. She could hear the sounds of men screaming for their lives, crying for God to save them, mixed in with the occasional burst of gunfire. Slowly, expecting to see the worst, Vicki gazed out from behind the crates toward the sounds of carnage.

A sea of white mist had overtaken the docks, much like the mists one would see hovering over the English moors on a tranquil Sunday morning. But there was nothing tranquil about the mist blanketing the docks in Harlem that night. Vicki and Louis were both witness to a slaughter. They saw men shooting into air, running in circles.... then being snatched into the mist by something…followed by a splash of blood and an abrupt end to the screaming. A scene played over and over again.

"I don't know what the hell I'm filming, Vicki," Louis says. I mean, I know what I'm seeing but…"

The reality of the situation finally set in for Vicki, and she spoke. "Let's get out of here, Louis. Now. Right now! Let's go!"

A blast of cold air startled Vicki. Suddenly in front of her, was a tall man standing to the side of Louis. With blood-red eyes…pale skin…and fangs. Once again, she was looking at a vampire.

Before she could scream again, the pale thing grabbed Louis from behind and threw him to the ground, forcing the camera to the floor. Vicki and Louis faced the tall creature standing before them, his blood-red eyes staring right at them. They expected a violent death, a loss of life, anything except hearing the creature talk.

"Go," the thing said to Vicki and Louis. "Both of you. Leave here. Now."

If one were to give Louis Tennio credit for anything, it would be for his strong sense of survival. Growing up in New York City taught him that when someone with the ability to kill you tells you to leave, you leave. Right away. No questions asked. So it was with this life-long sense of survival instilled in him that, after hearing the words of the undead thing standing in front of him, Louis took off running. Despite being in his mid-forties and many pounds overweight, Louis ran away from the scene with decent speed. One could almost forgive him for leaving Vicki behind, alone to face the dead thing in the mist.

Vicki was too frightened to look at Louis run away. She sat on the ground with her eyes fixed on a vampire. Every instinct in her body screamed for her to leave. Every sense of reason she had told her to get out of there, to follow the same words she said to Louis just minutes ago. And Vicki would leave, leave right now.

Except…. now that she had seen this thing stand in front of her in full view and had heard it speak…she was *curious*.

The reporter in her wanted to know what was going on. Her body was ready to run; her mind was ready to ask the creature a question. In this battle of wills, her mind won. Once Vicki Ramos made up her mind, there was no turning back. Even if it killed her.

"Who are you? Where did you come from?"

The pale thing was momentarily stunned. Hearing the human female ask him a question after he told her to leave was the last thing he expected. However, the feeling of surprise was quickly replaced with an all too human emotion. Anger.

"I told you to leave!" The thing moved toward Vicki and repeated his warning. "GO!"

The tension between curious human and deadly vampire was broken up before it could continue. "Marcus! We have to leave!" The thing turned at the sound of his name being called.

If Vicki were not so scared, she would've been ecstatic. She just picked up a seemingly very important piece of information, information she was not supposed to know. Vicki looked at the vampire. "Marcus?"

The dead eyes of Marcus turned toward her voice. For a second, their eyes met, and for that one second, Vicki could see a trace of humanity in Marcus' blood red eyes. A hint of a human life from a long time ago. Then he was gone. The mist quickly surrounded him, and Marcus disappeared.

There was nothing but silence now. Where there were sounds of death and dying and gunfire just minutes ago, there was now an eerie quiet. Vicki stood dazed, trying to register everything that had just happened. *Marcus. His name is Marcus. I've just escaped being killed by a vampire that has a name.*

The sound of sirens in the distance snapped Vicki from her thoughts. The police would be here soon, and she really didn't want to be the one to explain to them what just happened. Vicki shook her head to wake herself, and then started moving quickly. She searched for the camera that Louis dropped but couldn't find it anywhere. Vicki looked in front, behind, and all around the area where the camera was, to no avail.

"Son of a bitch," Vicki spoke in frustration. "That thing took the camera! Great. I go through all this shit and I don't even have a second of film to show for it!"

The sirens were getting louder, and Vicki knew she had to leave. Still cursing the loss of film, Vicki ran off toward the street. Incredibly, the news van was still parked in the same location. *Lucky thing I keep a spare set of keys. Louis must have hopped a cab or something.* Seconds later, Vicki was driving down 125th Street, away from the bloodshed and the death, away from where the police showed up moments later, away from where a vampire named Marcus spared the lives of her and Louis.

You have a name, Marcus. You have a name and I have a real good description of you, and that's all I need. I have a whole lot of questions to ask you, my friend, and I intend to get the answers. I just hope you don't kill me in the process.

CLUES

It had been daylight for almost an hour. Fifty-nine minutes after the first rays of sunlight shone through the dark morning sky. It was a sunny winter Saturday morning in New York City. Sitting on her bed, Vicki Ramos was awake to see it. However, beautiful sunrises were the furthest thing from her mind. Instead of appreciating the beauty of the dawn, she was appreciating the fact that she was alive.

Vicki drove home from the carnage of last night, stumbled into her apartment, crawled into bed, and proceeded to stay up the entire night. At first she tried to sleep, but it soon became clear that wasn't going to happen. All through the night, Vicki kept seeing images of what she had witnessed… the screams, the blood, the many dead bodies laid out like casualties of war, the mist which came and left. Finally, the cryptic warning by a vampire named Marcus. She could finally admit to herself that it *was* a vampire. Damn sure couldn't have been anything else. For some reason, she and Louis were given an opportunity to get out of there alive, an option that the drug dealers were never even presented with.

It's like they were on a mission. They went right after those guys and didn't give them a chance. We just happened to be at the wrong place at the wrong time. Usually that'll get you killed, but me and Louis were spared. Why? And to top it off, one of them has a name. Marcus. Tall, white, European-looking type, and oh yeah fangs, can't forget the fangs-

Vicki's phone rang, interrupting her thoughts. The office number of Nathan Tibbs showed up on her phone. Vicki went to answer, and then hesitated. They might want her to go out and cover the massacre of last night. *Hell no, I DO NOT want to go back there. Once is enough for me. Yeah, I want to find this Marcus, but I don't want to go back to that scene. I need some time to recover from this shit, and then look for him myself, on my terms.*

The ringing stopped, and a minute later a voice mail message icon appeared. Calling into her voice mail, she heard Nathan's message. "Vicki, its Nathan. Where the hell are you? We've been trying to reach you since last night. Cops found twenty-something bodies at the Harlem docks. I know you and Louis were out there, what the hell happened? We want to have you do a report for the morning show but I can't find you. Is your cell working? Get back to me ASAP!"

For the last three years, Vicki's career had been the top priority in her life next to her family. She sacrificed relationships, longtime friendships, and even turned down several offers from other stations to get to where she was. Normally, a call from Nathan was immediately picked up or responded to. But this time, Vicki let the voice mail go unanswered. She stayed on her bed, staring out the window, feelings of fear, commitment, and curiosity swirling within her. After a short while, Vicki got up from her bed to open all the blinds in her apartment, illuminating the entire place with sunlight. She made one phone call to her parent's house to let them know she'd be out all day. In reality, Vicki just wanted to be left alone. Curled up on her sofa, Vicki drifted in and out of sleep for the next few hours, her fatigue finally catching up with her while fear kept her from fully embracing slumber.

When Vicki fully awoke around noon, her entire apartment was awash in sunlight. Perhaps it was this total lack of darkness that emboldened her, or maybe it was her building anger at the situation. Either way, the Vicki Ramos that awakened was not the frightened woman from last night, but the feisty, hardheaded Latina she is usually known as. She rose from her sofa with a purpose, heading to the bedroom to fetch her phone. Sorting through her contacts, Vicki found a number and dialed it. Two rings later, a soft-spoken man named Warren answered.

"Hey handsome," Vicki chimed. "Remember me?"

"Hey, Boricua. Haven't heard from you in a while. What's up?"

"Oh, not much. Just recovering from a really bad night."

"Told you about that hard liquor. Or maybe you just smoked some good shit."

Vicki laughed at that comment. She could have used some good weed last night. "Nah, I wasn't that lucky. Listen, I need a favor…"

Warren breathed a heavy sigh. "See, that's all you call me for. Favors and tips. Not even gonna ask me how I'm doing or whether I'm single or if I wanna go out. Here I am, a nice, handsome, hardworking man, no trouble with the law, and you won't even consider my request for a date. Yet you call me about twice a year to get a tip. I feel so used. Maybe it's because I'm Jamaican."

"Oh, please Warren. You haven't been to Jamaica since you were five. You're as American as I am, child. You know I don't have time for dating or a boyfriend or anything like that. And I call you a lot more than twice a year, you're just never home. Maybe I would consider dating you if you weren't such a player."

"I'm only a player because I don't have you."

Vicki was momentarily stunned. After all the craziness of the past 12 hours, this was the nicest thing she could have heard. "Thank you, Warren. That was so sweet. You have no idea how much I needed to hear that. Listen honey, I really need a favor from you. You still have those contacts from around town?"

"Actually, I made some more friends last week. You

heard of that new club opening in Brooklyn? Those guys. It pays to be a club promoter, sweetheart."

"Nice! Ok, check this out. I'm looking for a guy named Marcus. Tall, about six feet, maybe two hundred pounds. White guy, probably European, with short light brown hair, and clean-shaven. Does that ring a bell?"

"Hmmm, that's some pretty vague information, Vicki. Do you have a last name or a hangout spot or anything else?"

"Nope. That's why I'm asking you. I was hoping you might have run into somebody or heard of someone like that with that name."

"Marcus you said, right? You know, I might know who you're talking about. My brother goes to that place down in the Village called The Chamber. They play hip-hop, dance, industrial, techno, all on different nights. You know Tommy; he listens to all kinds of music, so he'll go there at any night to hear whatever's playing. He went on Goth night last Wednesday, and saw some freaky-ass people up in there."

"Anyway, he was talking to some chick when this guy steps to her and tells her they got to go. Tommy's asking the girl if that's her boyfriend, and she says no, that he's just a friend and she ain't going anywhere. The guy grabs her arm and says, 'Marcus says we have to go.' Tommy told me that they both looked over by the door and there was this tall, white guy just looking at them, you know? Staring them down big time. The girl looks at Tommy and says, 'I gotta go,' then they left."

Vicki thought about the night before. It was a girl's voice that called out Marcus' name! She remembered that. "Did Tommy say anything about what this Marcus guy was wearing?"

"Not really. He said dude looked like Neo from The Matrix, so I guess he had a black trench coat or something. Tommy was pissed, too. He said he almost walked over to the guy to see what his problem was. Does that sound like your guy?"

"Yeah, that sounds like him, all right," Vicki said.

"Believe me, your brother did the smart thing not stepping to him. He is not someone to play around with. Just trust me on this one."

"Yeah, I figure if you're asking for all this info on him he must be up in some no-good business. You're not thinking of going down there on Wednesday night?"

"Warren are you saying you're worried about me? Vicki, the tough Puerto Rican mami from the Bronx? Sweetie, you're too kind, but I can take care of myself. I do appreciate your concern, though."

"You shouldn't go by yourself, if this guy is as bad you say he is. I'm supposed to go to this party in Newark that night, but I'll pass on it, so I can go with you."

Once again, Vicki was touched by what Warren said. "You're such a sweetheart, Warren. Don't miss your party. I'll bring someone with me, don't worry," Vicki said, not meaning a word of it. "Thank you so much for the info, baby. I owe you some nice cheesecake at Junior's."

"I'm down, but what I would really like is a nice date with you. You know, movies, dinner, candlelight at Coney Island, the whole nine. What do you say?"

"Hmmm, that does sound nice. Tell you what...I'll think about it, OK? And believe me, for me to even consider a date at this point in my life is a big step. But I will give it a lot of thought, I promise. Listen sweetie, I gotta run. Thanks for everything, Warren. I'll call you later this week and let you know how things went."

"All right, boo. You be careful and don't get all crazy out there. I want you to come back for our date." Warren couldn't help but smile as he spoke. "Let me know how things go."

"OK, Warren. Bye hon." Vicki hung up the phone and immediately her mind went to work. Wednesday night.

The Chamber. Oh yeah, it's on now. I'm gonna look for you, Dracula Jr., then you and I are gonna have a real talk.

THE LAIR

New York City had undergone a change of image since the 1970s. Where once The Big Apple looked like a city overrun by crime, decay, and neglect, the present day image of New York is of a safe, clean city, thriving with big business and new housing. There were more people actually moving into the city instead of moving away. Yet despite the cosmetic changes and the huge clean-up effort, there were still some pockets that could best be described as an abandoned ghetto. One such area was a building in the South Bronx. Old, decrepit, and almost fully empty, these structures could hardly be called 'housing.' The next to last building on this block was a perfect example; boarded windows, holes in the walls, and no fire escapes. At first glance it would appear to that no living thing could actually live in this place. But for the unliving, particularly a small group of immigrants from Yugoslavia, it worked just fine. This was the place they called home.

Up on the top floor, the walls separating the apartments had been knocked down to create one huge, open area. Remnants of what once belonged to previous residents lay strewn across the floor, or thrown in a bundle in one of the closets. The windows looking outside had been boarded shut, and then layered with black plastic wrapping. Not a ray of sunlight entered the area. Instead, the only light came from several gas lamps and candles.

Lying on the floor, taking up almost the entire space

of this open area, were five coffins. Unlike the colorful coffins one might find in a funeral parlor, these coffins were plain and crude, some beginning to splinter at the edges. They appeared as if they have been around for centuries, and indeed hey had.

The silence in the room was broken as the top of one of the coffins began to move. Slowly, the coffin lid rose in the air, a cold, dead hand pushing it from underneath, and the vampire known as Marcus rose up. Soon, the other coffins raised their lids and the other four vampires awoke; Alexander, Mila, Stephen and Gennedy. The sun outside began to set, meaning the day for these creatures had just started. The group headed to what used to be the living room, now an area where broken chairs and ragged sofas were the only furniture. They sat down and prepared to talk. Marcus, sitting by himself facing the others, spoke.

"We don't have much time. Our goal is within reach, but the humans are beginning to have suspicions. Although this culture doesn't believe we exist, it would be foolish to risk any more humans seeing us. We have to be careful from here on until we accomplish what we came here for."

"Speak for yourself, Marcus," replied Alexander. "If anyone should be careful about the humans finding out about us, it's you. First you tear up that blood bank, and then show yourself to those humans at the docks last night. They were recording the whole attack with a video camera. You see it, right? It's the one laying in pieces over there in the corner. So look in the mirror before you criticize. Oh wait, you can't look in the mirror. You're a vampire. Sorry!"

Marcus shook his head. "You really picked up this modern American sense of humor quite well, Alexander," Marcus said. "While you're going on about what I did, let me remind you who it was that left that body lying near Columbia University last week. Did you know they found a piece of his throat underneath a nearby car? Next time at least clean up after your meal."

"Dude, I licked all the blood off the street. I did everything right except I missed the throat piece. My bad. By the way, that blood was nasty. Worst I've ever had. I'm still feeling queasy, and that really shouldn't happen to a vampire. What kind of stuff was he on anyway? But you're right. I'll be more thorough next time. Hey, at least I didn't shout your name out for the world to hear." Alexander turned to look at the only female member of the group, a young looking vampire named Mila.

"That would be you, wouldn't it Mila? The little she-vamp with the loud mouth and baby brain. My dear undead bloodsucker, didn't it occur to you that saying his name around the humans might not be the smartest thing in the world to do?"

Mila turned her face away from Alexander, looking at the others for some sympathy. Petite and short, with cropped black hair and pale skin, she could easily pass for a teen Goth girl in any club. In fact, she was barely 16 when a she was turned from a sweet human child to a member of the undead. "I'm sorry. I didn't even know those people were there. I heard the police sirens and I panicked."

"Panicked?" says Alexander, in a sarcastic tone. "Wow, a human emotion. You really are further along than the rest of us, aren't you? Is it okay if we follow your lead so we can get there too?"

"Shut up, Alex," said Stephen, "Your smart-ass remarks aren't gonna get us any closer, either." A tall vampire with dark brown skin and a small Afro, Stephen was an American soldier stationed in the vampire's homeland. A late night out with friends ended up with them becoming vampire food and him being turned, like Marcus, into an unwilling member of the damned. Stephen's turn happened only several months earlier, making him the most recent addition to the clan. As a result, Stephen still held a great deal of resentment towards his existence as a vampire, and regularly took out his frustrations on the others.

"Still mad at being turned, Stephen? Well, cry me a fucking river. All I hear from you every day is your whining about being a vampire. Where you always such a crybaby as a human? Or is this one of those black things that I wouldn't understand?"

"That's enough!" Marcus yelled. Everyone stopped talking and faced him. Though it was never explicitly stated, Marcus was the de facto leader of the group. He wouldn't normally raise his voice, but when he demands their attention, he gets it. "That's enough from everybody. This isn't doing us any good. We're so close now; we can't afford to lose it by arguing with each other. What's done is done. We can't change the past. Alexander has the camera, and without that the humans have no proof we exist. Our main concern is the church."

Gennady spoke. "I agree, Marcus. The church should be our only concern now. There is no telling how much time we have before the humans discover us. Or worse, if we are discovered by him."

Gennady's words hung in the air. All five of them knew full well about "him," and they would much rather prefer facing the humans than facing him. All except Marcus. While he had no desire for them to be discovered, he had no fear of him. No, the fear that Marcus had was for another individual. A man who lived a long time ago, walking into a lake to be baptized…

"I should know about the church this weekend," said Marcus. "I'll know when it will be closed to the humans, and available to us. Until then, we've got to keep a low profile and stay clear of the innocents. Our time is coming. Let's not ruin everything we've tried to accomplish. The leaving, the sacrifice, the tainted blood. It will all be worth it when this is over."

Alexander nodded his head in agreement. "Well said, Marcus. Sorry if I offended you guys. I'll try to keep my witty remarks to myself. Anyway, I'm hungry. I'm gonna go find someone to eat." Alexander got up and walked toward the door, followed by Stephen and Gennady. Alexander put his arm around Stephen and laid his head on his shoulder.

"I'm sorry, soldier. Will you forgive me?"

"Only if you promise never to put your head on my shoulder again."

Gennady walks up to Stephen. "Be thankful he hasn't put his head anywhere else."

Mila finally stood up, and with her head hung low, walked toward Marcus.

"I'm sorry about last night," Mila said. "Please tell me I didn't endanger the mission. I want this to happen, Marcus. I want this so bad. I know you weren't happy with me for talking to that human in The Chamber last week, but at least I didn't mention your name. Please tell me that my mistake won't destroy us."

"You didn't endanger the mission, Mila. It's going to be OK," said Marcus, placing his hand on Mila's arm to show his support. "Besides, it's just a name. It won't do her any good. Let's be honest, it's not like she's going to come looking for me."

THE FAMILY RAMOS

Vicki Ramos sat her mother's kitchen table. In front of her, on a beautiful piece of fine china, lay a delicious Puerto Rican dish known as a *pastele.*

Made from crushed green bananas and stuffed with foods ranging from meat to rice to beans, then laid onto a banana leaf and tied with string, finally cooked in steaming water. The result was pure heaven as far as Vicki (and most Puerto Ricans) were concerned.

Digging her fork into the *pastele* on her plate, Vicki pulled off a slightly large chunk and plunged it directly into her mouth. She chewed her food slowly, taking the time to savor every piece of flavor. Making time to join her parents for dinner was a good decision indeed.

Seated next to Vicki was her mother Beatriz, while her father Hector sat at the head of the table. All were enjoying plates full of *pasteles, arroz con pollo, red beans* and *platanos.* Salsa music blared throughout the brownstone. This was home for Vicki. This would always be home.

Later on in the evening, Vicki sat on the sofa while her parents entertained the other guests who stopped by (promises of taking home food certainly helped).

I need to come back here more often. I keep forgetting that I'm their only child. I know Mami wanted more kids. I wish she would tell me she couldn't. Papi told me about her cancer. I was so mad she didn't tell me, but now I know why.

She didn't want me to worry. She knew I would've lost it if she had died. Typical Beatriz Ramos, always looking out for others instead of herself. And of course Papi made me swear never to tell her he told me. Like she made HIM swear never to tell me! How funny!

I should be more careful. I shouldn't be putting myself in crazy situations. Me getting killed would kill them. I can't do that to them.

But...

...dammit I can't help it. I was on such a high the other night. Being there to film that deal was like crack. Until Dracula and his posse showed up. Fucking ruined everything!

Now I gotta put myself out there again, just because I'm hard headed. No, it's because I wanna know who this freak is. What's his story? How is it possible for vampires to really exist? He's gonna talk to me. He owes me one.

But I really gotta be careful. I can't be the one to break my parents' hearts like that. Yo, if they only knew...!
How funny though...It's my turn now to keep a secret to protect someone's feelings.

Bueno, that's for later. Right now I'm hungry. Where's the flan?

VAMPIRE IN THE CORNER

Wednesday evening in the Bronx, and the sun was nowhere to be found. It was somewhere in the sky...night had not yet fallen...but was hidden behind gray skies and thick clouds. Which meant it was safe enough for Marcus to venture outside, albeit with a knit cap, scarf, gloves and sunblock on his face. Marching out in full sunlight was still a death sentence for the undead, but thanks to modern inventions such as sunblock and clothing made from different materials, a vampire could venture out before nightfall under the right conditions.

Marcus had been wanting to do this for a while now, since coming to America. But he had always held himself back. Mostly because he didn't want to disintegrate into ash. He had casually asked the other members if they wanted to try it, but they all quickly declined. Alexander replied with a long hearty laugh and walked off. Mila ducked under the covers. Stephen gave Marcus his usual look of derision. Gennady simply said "No."

Fashion played a role as well. *I'm going to look ridiculous going outside, wrapped up in 20 layers of clothes and covering my face.* But after much research about clothing materials, cloudy weather and SBF 50, Marcus was ready to make his move.

The clock turned 5:02 when Marcus stepped outside. Minutes passed as he waited. All that happened was feeling a little warmer than usual. A little uncomfortable, but nothing too serious.

I should be fine for 10-15 minutes. Enough time to check out the neighborhood.

And check it out he did. Three blocks from the lair was a corner store. Marcus had seen it many times before, always at night when it was closed. Now he could see it open for business. During the warmer spring, tables would be outside lined up with fruits, vegetables and sometimes fresh fish. Today though all the food was inside.

Marcus walked into the store. He was immediately struck by constant noise, a combination of chatter, price questions and loud humanity. This store was usually packed and today was no exception. Voices overlapping, different languages (Marcus picked out a French speaker), just normal hustle and bustle. Not too much different from the village market he used to go to as a child.

The vampire settled into a corner, standing quietly. For just a few minutes, he wanted to take in this activity. For just a few minutes, he wanted to feel human again. Alive. He took a deep breath, hoping his senses still had enough life to register the sensation. The full encounter evaded him, yet he was fortunate enough to detect a slight whiff of tobacco and bread. Strange combination indeed, but Marcus would take it. He took another breath and held it in. Savoring the few seconds of a sense that had been slowly coming back.

"Are you OK?"

Marcus opened his eyes and saw the owner of this voice. A little girl, no older than four, bundled in a pink jacket with a large hoodie, pink sweatpants and pink boots. She was looking at him with a look of slight confusion. The vampire smiled back at the little human, and replied in a reassuring tone.

"Yes, I'm OK. Thank you for asking."

"You looked like you were asleeping. You hafs to sleep in a bed.

"That's true. But I'm OK. I was just a little tired."

"Take a nap. Naps is good. My mommy makes me take a nap sometimes" She then mimics a snoring noise.

Marcus laughed. "That's a good idea. I'm gonna take a nap soon as I get home."

"Do you have a blankie?"

"Um, no. Should I get one?"

"Yah you should!" the little girl excitedly claimed. "I always sleep wif my blankie. Even when it stinks."

Marcus smiled, a big happy smile. The little girl smiled back, the type of pure innocent smile only kids can give. Had she been older, perhaps the girl could have seen past Marcus's smile and seen the pain in his eyes. Perhaps she could've asked him about the sadness behind the smile. Perhaps he would've told her about the many children he had encountered over the last 200 years, and how he had killed them all. Plunging his fangs into their necks and holding tight while their screams slowly faded. Some of them resembled this little girl. Same eyes, same expressions...same life. How many of them had blankies? How many of them were there, period? Perhaps he would've asked her for forgiveness for his sins, or to ask God to forgive them. But none of that happened. Instead it remained a chance meeting between a little girl and a monster trying not to be one.

Marcus refused to have this moment ruined by dwelling on the little lives he had taken. No, he would not dwell on those memories now. Not when a small child, the epitome of everything they came here for, told him things that made him smile.

The girl's mother, holding her daughter's hand and watching the interaction, paid for her groceries. She flashed a friendly smile at Marcus, then started to exit the store. The little girl waved at Marcus, and walked out with her mother, back to a home with a warm stinky blankie.

Twelve minutes passed, and the slightly uncomfortable warmth started getting warmer. It was time to go home. On his way back to the lair, Marcus spotted the little girl and her mother entering a building. He was relieved to know they made it home safe.

Later that night, Marcus exited his building. He had just received some important information, and had to be somewhere soon. Before leaving the neighborhood, he stopped at the building where the little girl lived. To assure his own feelings, Marcus wanted to make sure mother and daughter were safe. Kneeling on the fire escape, hiding in the shadows to avoid detection, he looked in the little girl's window. There she lay, sound asleep with her head half off the pillow...and a small blanket wrapped around her.

Marcus smiled, secure in knowing the little girl was home safe. The vampire then disappeared into the night, to where he was determined to once again meet a certain someone.

HELLO AGAIN

By the fifth day, Vicki Ramos couldn't wait anymore. It had been five days since the massacre at the docks, five days since she saw 26 men brutally murdered, five days since she came face to face with a monster. Tonight was the night she hoped to face this monster again, and she couldn't wait.

It didn't help matters that she had gotten in a lot of trouble at work. Her failure to film the drug deal like she promised, followed by her refusal to cover the dock massacre and to get in touch with Nathan all day Saturday would have meant career suicide for almost anybody else. It was only the fact that she was WABC's biggest name, as well as her exemplary work record that kept her employed. After her initial shock at the murders, she was able to focus on her job and wait patiently for Wednesday night to come.

Taking advantage of one her much-accumulated personal days (Vicki never asked for a day off in three years at the station) Vicki was able to get that night and the next day off, free and clear. She wouldn't have to worry about getting called for work or anything else, having visited her parents and siblings earlier in the evening. She even managed a quick check up on Louis (who the spent the entire visit apologizing for leaving her). Vicki's single-mindedness and determination were in full effect this evening. She was on the hunt for a vampire, and she was determined to find him.

Vicki stepped out of her apartment wearing a dark

brown leather jacket and matching gloves, with tight black jeans and a sweater underneath. Rounding out the outfit were boots and a few sprays of Tommy Girl perfume. *Warren would faint if he saw me in these jeans,* she thought. *Maybe I'll wear this on our date.*

Oh wow, I actually said "our date". Guess he's finally gonna get what he wanted. But that's cool. He earned it.

Not wanting to use her own car tonight, Vicki walked downstairs to catch the Uber waiting outside her apartment building and headed for The Chamber.

Her Uber pulled in front of the club and Vicki stepped out. The Chamber didn't look like too much from the outside, just a big door leading into a building, and a few cheap flyers taped outside. Then again, maybe that was the whole idea. Already, Vicki noticed that she was going to stand out.

I know its Goth night, but damn! Everyone here looks like they came from a Twilight marathon. I don't see any girls dressed like me. Now I see a few guys looking normal. I don't think Marcus will recognize me at first.

Vicki walked toward the door. Her flattering outfit drew a quizzical look from the bouncer, who nonetheless wasted no time waving her in.

This club was pretty much as Vicki imagined it would be. A dark warehouse with a few strobe lights shining through a smoky haze, heavy techno music pumping in the background. She ordered a drink, rejected an offer to buy some Molly, and settled into a corner where she could watch who left and entered the club. Five minutes passed. Ten minutes. Fifteen. Twenty. No sign of Marcus. *OK, this is not working. I'm gonna have to go out and hustle some info out of somebody.*

Vicki sauntered to the other side of the club, approaching a well-built man with long, brown hair pulled back into a ponytail. "Hi there! Listen, I'm sorry to bother you but I need your help. I'm supposed to meet this guy here on a blind date. His name is Marcus. I thought that maybe you might have seen someone that looks him. He's a pretty tall guy, taller than you. Slim build, light brown hair, and black clothing. Have you seen someone like that?"

The man in the ponytail looked at Vicki for a second, then in a monotone voice replied; "I don't know who you're talking about."

Jeez, when was the last time HE got laid? "Well, thanks anyway." Vicki flashed a fake smile then walked off. She didn't notice the man in the ponytail watching her as she walked away. Nor did she notice as he left toward one of the club's back rooms, pulling out his phone. And she had absolutely no knowledge that the man in the ponytail was a European vampire named Gennady.

Vicki asked a few other men if they've seen the tall man named Marcus. They all said no. She started to walk back to her corner when one of the guys she had asked approached her. "Excuse me; I think I've found your friend. He's out in the parking lot, through that back door. He says he was looking for you too."

Vicki was stunned. "Thanks," she replied before heading for the back door. *He's looking for me too? How does he know I'm here? Maybe he's a physic vampire.*

Normally, Vicki Ramos would have known better than to believe someone as readily as she believed this man. It might have been her single-mindedness about finding the vampire. Or it might have been her arrogance (I faced a vampire and lived, no punk is gonna scare me) but whatever it was, Vicki left all traces of common sense at home. Looking around to make sure no one noticed her, she slipped out the back door into a poorly-lit alley, shutting the door behind her (another stupid move she normally wouldn't do). "Hello?" she spoke into the darkness. "Marcus, are you here? Hello?"

"Sorry baby," a voice responded back to her. "Marcus ain't here." Suddenly, Vicki was grabbed from behind and shoved against the wall, several arms pinning her arms down. She tried to scream but another hand covered her mouth. Vicki attempted to ID her attackers, but it was too dark and she couldn't get a clear view.

I'm so fucking stupid! I survive a vampire and end up getting killed by some punk rapists. Oh God, they're reaching for my zipper…no, don't rape me…you mother fucker, don't rape me…

A thick, foggy mist made its way through the alley.

The hands she couldn't see trying to take off her pants belonged to the short, stocky guy who told her Marcus was outside. He and his two friends were determined to get some money tonight, and if they can take something else, then so be it. Vicki's struggling and kicking prevented the short guy from fully getting a firm grip on her jeans, and her fighting back was not in vain. As soon as he was finally able to get a firm enough grip to get her pants off, a dead hand reached out to grab the short guy by his scalp. Before he could even realize what was happening, the short guy was sent flying towards the back of the alley, hitting the trash bin with a loud thud.

Vicki stared in amazement. Standing in front of her was Marcus.

It's him! Holy shit, he's here! Oh God, these guys are dead.

Not wasting any time, Marcus grabbed one of the other attackers and slammed him into the wall with brute force, sending the man into unconsciousness. However, the last guy left did not panic. He quickly pulled out a gun and shot Marcus square in the back. The vampires' body lurched forward and slumped to the ground with a loud thud, no sign of motion or life evident.

"How you like that, motherfucker!" the guy screamed at Marcus' body. He turned and looked at Vicki with anger and murder in his eyes. For a split second Vicki believed she will die in this alley, she will be raped in this alley…but only for a split second. That's all it took for Marcus to swiftly rise up and grab the guy's hand holding the gun. In one swift motion, he bent his arm backwards and twisted it completely around, breaking the arm in three places. The would-be rapist screamed out in excruciating pain. Marcus clutched the guy's throat to silence him, and exposing his fangs, prepared to feast.

And indeed, this would be a feast that Marcus would long enjoy. Any coward who would rape a woman deserves this kind of death, he believed, and within seconds his blood would be running down Marcus' throat…

"No! Don't kill him!" Vicki yelled.

Stunned, Marcus looked at her, his face one of utter confusion. It was the second time in five days that Vicki had said something to confuse the hell out of him.

"Just leave him there, OK? You don't have to kill him."

Marcus looked back at his intended victim. The guy who was so tough thirty seconds ago now cried out in pain begging for his life. The bloodlust raged within Marcus, but Vicki's pleas made him hesitant. Dammit! Why was she doing this? Suddenly the familiar sound of police sirens was heard, and Marcus knew that they must depart.

First though, Marcus slammed his intended victim's head into the hard floor. *If I can't kill him my way, maybe I'll crack his skull,* Marcus thought. He then quickly grabbed Vicki by her arm, brought her close to him and leaped high into the air. It all happened so fast for Vicki that it took her a moment to realize the vampire holding her tight was not leaping anywhere… THEY WERE FLYING.

She managed to catch a bird's eye view of the buildings beneath her. She couldn't tell how high she was, nor did she care to find out. It was all she could do to keep from losing her mind.

This can't be happening, she thought. *THIS CANNOT BE HAPPENING!*

Vicki kept her eyes closed throughout the entire flight, which lasted less than thirty seconds. She suddenly felt something solid under her feet. The flying was done, and she was on a solid surface. Opening her eyes, Vicki saw her feet placed firmly on a rooftop. Slowly her senses returned to normal, and she began to calm down after that nerve-wracking flight. Marcus stood a few feet away from her, facing the other way. He turned and spoke to her. "Are you all right?"

Physically, Vicki was fine. No gunshots, no teeth marks, a few bruises from the struggle. Emotionally, she was terribly shaken. Coming within seconds of being raped was bad enough, but actually flying through the air would've been enough to drive most people straight to Bellevue. Vicki certainly came close to losing it, but managed to keep it together. Scared as she was, she DID accomplish her goal tonight: Find Marcus the Vampire. For the second time in less than a week, Vicki put a brave front on her fear to focus on the moment at hand.

"Uh yeah, I'm fine," Vicki answered, still slightly shaken. "Really, I am. Hey, it's not every day you get to fly over Manhattan without FAA approval. That's a neat little trick you got. Thanks for helping me back there."

"That's the second time this week I've saved your life. You're beginning to become a habit. And I don't even know your name."

"Oh, it's Vicki. Vicki Ramos. I don't know if you watch TV but I'm a pretty famous reporter for Channel 7 news."

"I tried to watch television once but all I saw were people cursing and fighting on a stage while someone named Maury kept telling people they were the father. Not worth my time." Marcus walked closer to Vicki. "You stopped me from feasting."

"You mean that guy? I'm sorry; it's just that I think killing someone is wrong. I mean, yeah I was pissed at him and he deserved to be punished but I didn't want him dead. Breaking his arm and scaring the hell out of him was enough. Killing him would have gone too far."

"Then he shouldn't have attacked you. Those who wish to live long should do the right thing."

"Listen to you. You sound like a commercial."

"I don't have time for this." Visibly annoyed, Marcus turned to leave. Vicki grabbed his arm, quickly and forcefully.

"Don't you leave yet! I didn't go through all this shit for nothing, just so you could up and fly away. I've been looking for you all night."

Marcus shot Vicki a serious stare. "So I was told. You're going to tell me why. I spared you and your friend the other night, yet you came back tempting fate. Didn't you see what happened at the docks?"

"Believe me, I saw it. But me and my friend were allowed to live. I want to know why, and I want to know why there's a bunch of vampires running around in my hometown. I have family here, you know."

"These are things you don't need to know. It doesn't concern you."

"Bullshit!" yelled Vicki, her anger now boiling over. Her façade was beginning to crack. Watching drug dealers massacred, getting yelled at by her boss, a near sexual assault, an unexpected flight that scared her half to death…all the events of the past week led up to her cursing at the man (vampire) she'd been searching for. Vicki just about had enough, and being told that everything that happened was none of her business was enough to set her off.

"You go around killing everybody except me? I think that would concern me. You save my life twice and then drag me to this rooftop? I think that would concern me. You want to know why I was looking for you? Because I want to know what the hell is going on here. So be a nice little vampire and please answer my questions, *Marcus*!"

The vampire came face to face with Vicki. Her saying his name with a heavy dose of attitude quickly turned his annoyance with her into anger. Marcus wasn't exactly having the best week ever either. All the years he spent as a vampire did not prepare him to deal with a human who refused to run away scared. Even worse, she asked questions!

"Don't push your luck, lady. You've been more fortunate than any other human I've known. Be satisfied you're alive and forget about what you've seen. Don't make me kill you."

Vicki looked back into Marcus' face with a defiant look. "At the risk of sounding cocky," she said, "you haven't killed me yet."

Without warning, Marcus clutched Vicki's throat and slammed her to the ground, exposing her soft fleshy neck. Vicki was overcome with fear, a look of sheer horror etched on her face. This time she really did go too far. For the second time that night she knew that she was going to die. Marcus bared his fangs and prepared to feast… but then stopped. His sharp teeth an inch away from Vicki's neck, he looked into her eyes. Marcus saw the fear on her face and froze for a moment. Though the bloodlust was raging, it was easy for him to stop; he really didn't want to kill her.

Shaking with fear, Vicki slowly pulled up her hands toward the vampire's face and made a cross sign with her fingers, hoping that this Hollywood trick would work in real life.

Marcus looked at her hand-made cross for a second, and as quickly as it came, the anger disappeared from his face. He looked at Vicki with a slight smile. "You need a real one," he told her. Slowly, Marcus pulled away from her, and walked away.

Vicki pulled herself up from the ground, frightened but feeling that the worst was over. She put her hand to her throat to reassure herself that everything was still there and functional. This time, she really had escaped certain death. But why did he stop? What had saved her? Vicki wanted to know but she wasn't about to ask Marcus right now. She already pushed her luck once tonight and that was more than enough. They both stood there for several minutes, neither one saying a word. Finally, Marcus spoke, visibly struggling to control his bloodlust.

"You've never been closer to death. I've spared lives these past few months, but never have I….," his words trailed off. Marcus walked over to an air conditioning duct and sat down, his head hung low.

After a moment, Vicki walked over and sat next to him. Scared as she was, her curiosity could not be denied. If he was going to kill her, there was nothing she could do about it.

Figuring it wouldn't hurt to sit and talk, Vicki walked over and carefully sat down next to her two-time savior.

She actually felt safe with him at this moment. Whatever rage he had was gone, as he sat peacefully. Marcus could not explain it, but her presence seemed to calm him. Looking out toward the night sky, Marcus told his story.

"I was like you once. Human. A child of God. Born Marcus Mikhail Burgov, February 1, 1791. A native of what's now called Yugoslavia. I remember the night that changed clearly, like it happened yesterday. I was 22 years old. I spent the whole day with the woman I had planned to marry, Ilana. We were running through the fields of the forest, two young fools madly in love. The moon was shining in the sky. We both fell down on the grass, and embraced. I still remember her lips…soft like silk."

"It was then I noticed a mist surrounding us, a frigid mist that appeared from nowhere. Suddenly, a hand reached out from the mist and snatched Ilana from my arms. I ran after her but couldn't see anything. I heard her screams, and I tried to follow them but I was lost in the mist. She had stopped screaming and I feared the worst. That's when a hand clutched my throat, forcing me to the ground. I felt a heavy weight on me. I tried to scream, to get up, but I couldn't. All I could do was feel the fangs pierce into the side of my neck. I blacked out, and I was convinced that I had died. In a way, I was right."

"It was some time after that I awoke in a dark cave, lying on a cold concrete slab. I remember feeling different. Alive, but not quite the same, as if I were an empty shell. All around me were dozens of people… vampires… and standing in front was a tall, older one. He was an elder vampire named Vladimir, and he was their leader. I discovered that I was chosen, along with my friend Alexander, to become members of an underground clan of vampires that had lived in Eastern Europe for centuries. They moved from country to country every hundred years, feasting off the populace and choosing a select few to join the clan, replacing those who had been exterminated by humans."

"Oh my God," said Vicki. "What happened to your girlfriend? Did she become a vampire too?"

"No. She was murdered. Since I was nowhere to be found, I assume the townsfolk believed that I was the one who killed her. I don't know what happened afterward, what hatred might have existed between our families. I don't know how much my parents suffered. I also don't know why I was chosen and not her. It was never explained to me. You see Vicki, there are many differences between vampires and elders. A vampire can kill a human but can't turn one into a vampire. Only an elder can do that. So while Ilana was attacked by vampires, an elder attacked me. Vladimir. Again, I'm not sure exactly why. The one time I asked him I was rebuffed. Forcefully, I might add. Since that night, I've been a member of the undead, feasting on the blood of the living."

Vicki looked at Marcus with a tinge of fear. "Is that why you came to New York, to build another clan?"

"That's what Vladimir thinks," Marcus replied. "We were actually supposed to go to Paris to do that. The truth is that I've come here, along with several of my fellow vampires, to find salvation. As long as we remain vampires, our souls are kept in purgatory. We want to find salvation from God, The Son Jesus Christ, and the Holy Spirit, so that our souls can find eternal peace in Heaven. That's why you, your friend, and many others have been spared. You are what we call innocents. Humans who harbor no evil within their souls. In other words, good decent people. However, we're still vampires and we still need to consume human blood to exist. Being that we're creations of evil, we can sense when a human is evil, when darkness resides deep inside their souls. These humans are the ones we hunt."

Vicki's face began to light up. "I get it. You still need to drink blood, but you don't want to commit any more murders because you're trying to get to Heaven. So you stay away from innocent people and only kill bad, evil people."

Marcus actually smiled. "You're right. It's our way of

asking for forgiveness for the countless lives we've taken. According to Judeo-Christian beliefs, once you are 'born again' and accept Christ as your savior, you make a conscious attempt not to sin anymore. That's exactly what we're doing. We haven't killed an innocent in the eighteen months we've been here in America."

"Accepting Christ as your savior. That's a good start. How do you plan on doing that?"

"Besides praying? I have something I'm working on." Vicki was very curious as to what that something might be, but she decided against pressing the issue. If he wanted her to know what it was, he'd tell her. "I just hope what we do will work. There are no promises, no guarantees. But I'd rather die trying than be condemned to an eternity of walking the earth as an undead bloodsucker."

Vicki shook her head. Although she knew that Marcus spoke the truth, and she had seen these creatures with her own eyes, it was still too much to take in all at once. Vicki's worldview just got a lot bigger. "You said that this Vladimir guy thinks you're here to start another clan," she asked. "What if he finds out what you're really up to? He's not gonna be too happy about it."

"What would happen…," Marcus replied, his words trailing off. "Remember what I told you earlier about elders having powers that vampires don't have? A vampire is a powerful creature. We have great strength, agility, and we're not easy to exterminate. But an elder is much more powerful. They have control over the elements, animals, and weak-minded humans. Powers of flight and levitation. Psychic senses. I could go on, but I'm sure you get the point."

"Is there anything you can do against an elder?" asked Vicki. "Throw garlic at him or something. How do you kill him?"

"We don't. A vampire can't kill an elder. Even if I managed to drive a stake through Vladimir's heart, he'd laugh and swat me away like a fly. The same power that Satan granted to all elders is the same power that protects them from other vampires. They can't be killed by another creation of evil. Only a child of God, a human, can kill an elder. That is, if a human were able to get close enough without getting killed. Over the centuries, many brave souls have tried to kill an elder. Many have failed. I've never heard of nor seen a human who managed to accomplish the deed, not since I've been a vampire." Marcus manages a small, sincere laugh. "And I don't think there's enough garlic in this city to make much of a difference."

Vicki laughed along with Marcus. She almost forgot she was talking to a vampire. *It's funny. I never would have imagined a vampire would be so human. He still remembers his human emotions and feelings. He's more open about his life than some living people I've met! I wonder if the others are like that. He even has a sense of humor about this.*

"Marcus, I know I went after you really hard to get some answers, but there was no way I could have gotten all this information from you unless you wanted me to know. I guess I'm just wondering why you decided to tell me."

Marcus faced Vicki, contemplating his answer. "I don't know. I trust you, and I know that you'll keep all of this a secret. Don't ask me how I know, I just do. Why does one open their heart to a stranger? Why does someone say 'I love you'? There is no answer. Even in death."

Marcus then stood, pulling Vicki up with him. "Time to go. I have to be somewhere soon. Where would you like me to take you?"

"Near my apartment would be fine," Vicki said, slightly disappointed that the conversation with Marcus is over. "Preferably not on the rooftop."

Marcus cracked a slight smile. *I've smiled more tonight than I have since I lost my human life. This woman stirs something in me. Something which shows me that our quest can be attained.*

Twenty minutes later, Vicki stood in front of her apartment building, having taken another flight with Marcus. The vampire walked her to the front door, and spoke. "Thank you for a nice evening. It certainly was not what I was expecting." Though still a little shaken, she felt more comfortable around Marcus. She tried hard not to smile too much. "Thank you, Marcus. Maybe we should try it again sometime. You know where I live." She opened the front door, then turned to speak to Marcus.

"Apartment 6E. Try not to come by on an empty stomach." With that, Vicki entered her building, leaving Marcus with his thoughts as he flew off into the night.

Apartment 6E. I'll remember.

PERDITION (Genesis)

Somewhere across the Atlantic, a telephone rang. A phone call transmitted from America reached the mainland of the United Kingdom, traveling through thousands of miles of cables from England to Eastern Europe until it reached its destination in Sarajevo. A pale, dead hand picked up the ringing phone, and a female voice speaking fluent Serbian answered.
"Hello."

"Vladimir."

"He is busy conversing with the creator. He demanded that he not be disturbed."

"Then give him this message. I have found the lost ones. I'm calling to let him know where they are. They are not ready to come home."

"Our master has been waiting for this. Where are you?"

"America. New York City."

FATHER MURRAY

The church in lower Manhattan was quiet on this night. Sunday evening mass had finished an hour earlier, and church pastor Arthur Murray was putting away the artifacts he had used this night. Father Murray was a seventy-four-year-old native New Yorker, born and raised in Brooklyn. He grew up watching Jackie Robinson play for the Dodgers (back when they were the real Dodgers, not the pale imitation paying in Los Angeles), and then going to games at Shea Stadium in Flushing, Queens to see the Mets (because no Dodgers fan could EVER root for the Yankees). Baseball was his passion until he reached his late twenties, when it gave way to the priesthood.

Arthur was one of the few kids in his neighborhood genuinely excited about going to church on Sundays. As an adult, he had tried several jobs but kept feeling the pull of the church calling him. He had tried living the so-called "American Dream" that most of secular America had wanted; getting married right out of college, getting a job, talking about kids, etc. Despite all of that, Arthur always felt something was missing. Except for the times he went to church. It was there, in the grace of God Himself, where he felt at home. Where he felt he belonged.

So when his wife had once again started arguing about their inability to keep up with the Joneses, Arthur Murray had an epiphany. He was tired of killing himself to please everyone in his life. If he were going to sacrifice himself for anything, it would be for God. Arthur announced his decision to become a priest.

Of course, celibacy is a vow for a Catholic priest, which meant Arthur had to tell his wife that he was leaving her. Mrs. Murray was shocked but relieved at the same time, as if she was now free to find the type of man who could give her the life she really wanted. Arthur wished her well and headed to his church, where he started on the long road that had been calling him.

That had been over forty years ago. Arthur Murray had no regrets at all, though there were times when he struggled with his celibacy. He was still a man after all. Nonetheless, he made his vow and had been true to it. This was his calling, and he was proud to serve the Lord. Besides, he still had baseball. He was looking forward to catching a few Mets games this season. Lord knows their bullpen could use all the divine help it could get.

All the church items had been put away, all the doors were locked, and all candles were put out. His work done for the night, Father Murray stepped out into the cold night air. Since his apartment was on the same block as the church, the walk home was always quick.

The priest suddenly felt a presence near him. A presence that was becoming more familiar. Right away he knew exactly who it was.

"Hi Marcus."

Father Murray was facing an alley to his right, looking upward at a fire escape. There, perched like a bird of prey (or an angel) was Marcus.

"Good evening, Father Murray. It's good to see you."

"Good to see you too, although I wish you'd pick an easier way of getting my attention. You're liable to give me another heart attack."

The old priest wasn't kidding. The first time they met, Father Murray was so frightened he suffered cardiac arrest, thereby prompting the only time in history that a vampire performed CPR on a human.

"Sorry about that. I tend to do that a lot. Force of habit, I guess."

"You're a vampire. It comes with the job." The priest smiled at that line. He felt this vampire was more human than he thought he was. Marcus paused for a moment, and then spoke. "It's time. We're ready."

"I've been waiting for you to give me the word. Tuesday night after mass will be the perfect time. I can close up the church and we'll have all the time we need."

Father Murray paused for a moment. "Marcus, I want you to know that I'll do my very best to help you and your friends, but I can't make any promises. There's no guarantee that this is going to work. I don't think anyone has ever attempted this before. I can't even guess what's going to happen. All I know for certain is that God loves and forgives."

"I understand, Father," Marcus replied. "I know I'm asking a lot. You've been blessing humans for so many years, helping others be closer to God, and now a bunch of vampires are asking you to bless us in a church so we can get to heaven. I just want you to at least try. Honestly, I don't even know if we'll be able to make it inside the church."

"YOU did," said Father Murray. "I have faith, Marcus. With God, all things are possible. You and your friends are proof of that. I've dedicated my life to helping others, and I'm not about to stop now."

"Thank you, father. Tuesday night might be the last time we ever walk this earth. You're a good person to spend their last moments with. I wish there was something we could do to thank you for all you've done."

"No need to thank me, son. This is what I do."

"I'll go tell the others. See you Tuesday night, Father. Take care, and God bless.'

"God bless you, Marcus." With that, the vampire leapt off the fire escape and disappeared into the night. Father Murray continued his walk home, contemplating the huge step he was about to undertake.

"Heavenly Father, grant me the strength and wisdom to complete the task ahead of me. I know you have faith in me. You brought me these lost souls for a reason. But I'm going to need as much help as you can give me, Lord."

IF YOU'RE EVER IN THE NEIGHBORHOOD...

The loveseat in Vicki's living room was a good place for her to sit. Despite the cold weather outside, her window was open. Vicki welcomed the cold air this night. She hoped it would clear her head, because lately a clear head was something she didn't have.

Vicki wasn't used to having a muddled mind. Not her. Part of the reason for her career success was her razor-sharp focus on the task at hand. She was given permission to film the drug deal on the docks partly because upper management trusted her to keep a level head and not let the magnitude of the moment overwhelm her. Vicki could handle anything that was thrown at her, until recently. This new situation was something she didn't see coming, and she wasn't quite sure how to deal with it.

The funny thing was it wasn't so much that Vicki had twice been saved (and once almost killed) by a vampire named Marcus, a creature that by all means shouldn't exist. Granted, that was one hell of a throw from left field, but what was really messing up her head was that for the past few days, she couldn't stop thinking about him. His face, his words, were constantly on her mind, and for one good reason:

She liked him.

Among her many good traits was Vicki usually being honest and open with herself. This night that honesty caused her emotions to spill forth, forcing her to have a seriously much needed conversation with herself.

I can't believe this. What the hell happened to my life? I'm sitting here with a fucked-up head, because of him. I like him. Jesus, I actually like this guy. I feel like I'm back at P.S. 28, like a little girl with a crush. I miss him! I gave him my apartment number, and he hasn't come by yet, and I wish he would. What the hell is wrong with me? What are you gonna do Vicki, get romantically involved with him? Mami and Papi would love that! HE'S NOT EVEN ALIVE!! I'd be having sex with a dead person. CAN we have sex? How can he get it up if he's dead? Dammit, if he can fly, he can fuck.

I'm freezing my ass off in my own place because I'm waiting for him to come here. Just come flying in my window, like Superman. A Superman Dracula.

Vicki chuckled at that thought, a mixture of laughter and sadness. She wiped the beginnings of tears from her eyes, stood up and sighed.

I need a drink.

"Hello Vicki."

The words hit her like a ton of bricks. For a split-second she thought she imagined hearing them. But his voice was clear and strong and unmistakable, and it was coming from her window. Quickly turning to face that voice, Vicki saw him standing there. Marcus the vampire had come to pay Vicki Ramos a visit. Superman Dracula was here.

"Oh! Hi!' Vicki managed to at least get those words out. She was shocked, surprised and happy to see him. Suddenly her mind was a lot clearer. "You remembered."

"Yeah. 6E. Pretty easy number. I hope I didn't scare you by coming in this way. I always liked a dramatic entrance."

"That's OK. The entrance fits you."

"You must be freezing."

Vicki nodded. She was in fact so cold her teeth were chattering. Marcus closed her window, and then stepped closer to where Vicki was standing.

"Step into my arms," Marcus said. "I'll keep you

warm."

Vicki didn't mean to, but she couldn't help it: she laughed out loud. Though she was touched by Marcus' intent...she did indeed want to him to wrap his arms around her...what he said and the way he said it was just too damn funny.

Marcus looked perplexed. "Did I say something wrong?"

"No sweetie, I'm sorry. You haven't talked to too many girls lately, have you?" Vicki moved closer to Marcus. "Actually, it was beautiful."

"You're welcome. You make it easy."

Both of them stood in silence for a moment, looking at each other and smiling. Vicki looked into Marcus' eyes, searching for something other than the pure evil that created him. What she found was a flicker of humanity, a spark struggling to once again burn bright within him.

Vicki tried to remind herself that it was only a short time ago when she looked into those same eyes and saw nothing but murderous, demonic rage, and she would do well to remember that.

Just a few minutes ago, she was crying and confused about her feelings for this creature but now he stood right in front of her, stood there like a fallen angel hoping to spread his wings and again fly to the heavens. It was all so clear. She had feelings for him, and she didn't want that to stop.

Vicki was not the only one undergoing emotional gymnastics. A swell of long dormant feelings stirred within Marcus. Strong and fast they came, threatening to overwhelm him, and for the first time since being turned into a vampire Marcus had to struggle to keep his composure. Marcus had tried to put it into words what he was feeling but came off sounding like a lovesick 13 year old. He was embarrassed, again another emotion he hadn't felt since losing his humanity. Marcus certainly wasn't used to being in this position, and wondered if he looked as harried as he felt.

She can't see me like this. I'm standing here trying not

to fall apart. She might get the wrong idea and think I'm going to hurt her. That's the last thing I ever want to do. Look into my eyes my darling and see that.

He can't see me like this. I'm standing here grinning like an idiot. He might get the wrong idea and think I'm afraid he's gonna hurt me. That's the last thing I want. I trust you, Marcus. Look into my eyes and you'll see that.

Several seconds passed before the silence was broken by Vicki's voice.

"Would you like something to drink? I'd ask if you were hungry but the only blood I have to offer is my own, and I kind of need it."

She always says something to make me smile. "Don't worry, I'm not hungry. Besides, I could never hurt you. Anything you got would be fine."

He could never hurt me. I believe him. He saved my life twice and stopped himself from feeding on me. You're my protector, baby. Vicki walked to her kitchen and retrieved a bottle of Bacardi rum. After walking back to her living room, Vicki and Marcus took their drinks and sat down on her sofa, very close together.

"Hope you like rum. I was all out of vodka."

"Rum is good. I've developed a taste for it recently. Never had the chance to drink it when I was alive."

"Do vampires get drunk?"

"I never have, not yet. Maybe this would be the rum to do it. Can you imagine me getting drunk and trying to fly out of here?"

"Don't let the cops bust you," Vicki said laughing.

"Yeah, they'd give me a FUI: Flying Under the Influence!" Marcus laughed heartily.

Vicki downed her drink. "Can you dance?"

Marcus thought for a second. "Dance? I guess...I've never really danced before. There were no dance clubs when I was growing up."

"I'll teach you." With a devilish grin, Vicki went over to her stereo. She looked underneath until she found what she wanted, her stack of vinyl records. Picking the one she wanted, she placed the LP on her record player. "My papi got me this last year. An actual record player. Seriously old school, I know! But I love the way these sound, especially with THIS song."

Vicki placed the needle on the record like an old pro, and the speakers blared out the classic slow jam THAT'S THE WAY OF THE WORLD by Earth Wind & Fire. Vicki offered her hand to Marcus as an invitation to dance. He smiled at her, took her hand, then stood and leaned close to her. Now he finally had his arms around her, as she wrapped hers arms around him, and the pair slow danced to the music.

"So, this is dancing. I can get used to this."

"You better. I love to dance, so I need a man who can keep up with me."

"I've heard this song before, somewhere. Nice music. The way of the world, indeed. Sometimes things are beyond your control. I hope that's not an omen."

Vicki hadn't thought of that. Didn't really want to. She wanted to hold onto him and not let go, just keep dancing. But the reality was inescapable. She savored this moment for a few minutes, just holding him and committing this moment to memory.

"This can't last between us, can it?"

Marcus sighed. He also knew the situation. This was what finally made him come to her place. Marcus wanted to see her, to hold her, because he might never get to do so again.

"I have to tell you something. This may be the last time we spend together."

Vicki looked deep into Marcus' eyes. "What do you mean?'

"Vicki, remember what I told you the other day? The other vampires and I came here to find salvation. We left our home and travelled across the ocean to try to save our souls. Tuesday night, all of us are going to a church in lower Manhattan. We're going inside the church to be prayed over and baptized by Father Murray, a friend of mine. I... I don't know what's gonna happen. No one knows. Maybe the curse will leave us and we'll live human lives, maybe we'll die burning or we'll turn to ash. I don't even know if our souls can be saved. It's a risk, but it's one we have to take. If we stay the way we are, I know how we'll end up, doomed to walk the earth forever, or until somebody puts a stake in our hearts. I can't deal with that anymore, my darling. Even though I've found someone who wants me to keep going."

Although Vicki was expecting something like this would happen, she didn't expect it so soon, right now. Just as they were starting to get closer, she was going to lose him.

"Are you sure this is what you want?"

Marcus took a deep breath. "Yes. I'm hoping, I'm praying, that we get to live on. I don't want to lose you. I want to enjoy the life that was taken from me. This is the only way I know to possibly make that happen. Not just for me, but my friends as well. We risked everything for this." Marcus caressed Vicki's hair, then kissed her softly on her forehead. "Please understand. Please know that being with you has made me feel alive again. You make me happy, Vicki."

"You make me feel good, too," Vicki replied, trying not to shed a tear. She then remembered something he had just said. "Did you say you have a friend named Father Murray? Your friends with a priest? How'd you pull that off?"

"I had been checking out several churches in the area. I wanted to enlist the help of a man of the cloth, someone who was especially close to God. My idea was if a real priest could help us, it would be legitimate. I saw Father Murray one night walking home from his church, and I was immediately drawn to him. His aura was so pure, so good-hearted. I knew he could be someone I could trust. I spoke with him just now, and everything's ready to go."

"Is that why you came by to see me? To tell me good-bye?"

"I came by because I wanted to see you. I want to spend time with you while I know I can. It's not time to say good-bye yet," Marcus smiled.

'Damn right it's not." Vicki replied. Without even

thinking of it, Vicki kissed Marcus...and Marcus kissed her back. For the first time in over 200 years, he tasted the lips of a woman. The flicker of humanity left in him exploded into a burning flame, and for this moment he was more human than bloodsucker. He embraced Vicki close, his body against hers. Marcus did not know how far this could go, but he was willing to see it all the way there.

Vicki, however, knew exactly where this was headed.

"Come with me," she said. Holding Marcus' hand, she started leading him to her bedroom. It didn't take Marcus long to figure out what the next step was.

"Vicki, I... I don't know if I can do this."

"Yes, you can, baby," she said, kissing him. "Yes you can."

Marcus honestly didn't know if he could perform sexually. But he was damn sure willing to find out. Giving in to his desire, he let Vicki lead him to her bedroom, to her bed, where he soon found the definitive answer to his question.

Yes, he could.

PERDITION (The Coming)

Sheila Germain wasn't looking forward to this flight. Not after getting a peek at who was flying with her.

Sheila was a flight attendant with Virgin Airways. Growing up in Michigan didn't give her much of a chance to get out and see the world, which was her goal in life since she was a little girl. Throughout her adolescence, she pondered what type of career she should embark on which would allow her enough money to travel at her leisure. Then Sheila had a bright idea. Why not become a flight attendant for an international airline? Not only would she be flying all over the world, she'd get paid nicely to do so. Her dream became reality, and for the last eight years she had indeed flown all over the globe. Sheila loved her job, usually. Today, not so much.

She first noticed something wrong the minute she stepped on the plane. Everyone was quiet, and for some odd reason the first-class section looked empty. Not just empty, but dark. Pitch black, almost. All the windows were completely covered to allow no sunlight in, and a heavy tarp was placed over the entrance.

Sheila wondered what was going on and went straight to the other senior attendant on duty, Ivy. Both were standing at the front of the plane, a few feet away from the darkened section. "Hi Ivy. What's the deal with first class?"

Ivy, looking a little nervous, replied. "Some rich guy

bought up the whole section for himself."

This was not completely uncommon. Sheila had heard of other wealthy passengers doing this on other flights. The darkness, however…

"But why is it so dark in there?"

"I was told he has some sort of skin condition. He's really sensitive to sunlight. The guy paid extra to have us black out the whole section."

"Is he here yet?" Sheila asked.

Ivy replied by nodding her head towards the very dark first-class section. The rich passenger with the skin condition was already seated. So dark was his seating area that Sheila missed him the first time she looked. When she finally did catch a glimpse, she wished she had kept on missing him.

Even sitting in his seat, he looked tall. A black fedora rested on his head, sunglasses covered his eyes, and a black scarf covered the rest of his face. A black winter coat and black gloves filled out the rest of his attire. It was as if The Phantom of the Opera had come to life. Every time Sheila looked at him, she felt a queasy feeling in her gut. She considered herself an atheist, but if there was ever a time she felt like converting to a major religion, this was it.

Ivy noticed the look on her co-worker's face. "Creepy, isn't he?" she whispered. "I can't look at him without feeling like I'm going to throw up. For once, I'm glad I don't have the first-class shift."

Sheila felt even sicker. "Don't tell me I have to serve this section today," she whispered, almost too loud.

Ivy shrugged her shoulders. She did feel bad for Sheila, who was a nice girl, but she didn't like her enough to switch places with her right now.

"Sorry, redhead. This was set beforehand. It could've easily been me."

Yeah, except it ISN'T you. "Well, shit." Sheila sighed. This was her job after all, and she was expected to be a professional. Putting on her happy face, she walked into first class and approached the passenger.

Though there was nothing outwardly wrong with him...he smelled of old cologne and his clothes were in perfect condition... Sheila still couldn't help but feel uneasy being this close to him. "Good day to you, sir. I want to welcome you aboard Virgin Airways. My name is Sheila and I'll be your attendant on this flight. Is there anything I can get for you?"

The passenger looked straight ahead and gave his reply in a thick Eastern European accent. "Wine. Red." It was the voice of someone who had obviously lived a long time, thick and gravelly. It almost didn't sound human.

"I'll get that for you right away, sir," Sheila replied. She wanted to run to the wine cabinet, then to the door and finally out of the whole damn airport, but she settled for walking briskly out of first class. Ivy was there to greet her.

"What's wrong? Is he that bad?" Ivy whispered. Both women were careful to not talk too loudly.

"He's just...weird. I don't know what's wrong with that guy, but he gives me the heebie jeebies. He acts like he's Count Dracula."

"Let's get him what he needs and hope he falls asleep," Ivy replied, "It's a long flight."

Sheila agreed with that. Overseas flights were usually eight hours long or more, so most passengers slept through it. Sheila hoped that's what her creepy passenger would do.

"Who knows, maybe he brought a coffin on board," Ivy joked, and both women shared a quiet laugh. Feeling a little better, Sheila prepared the glass of wine, Ivy began her flight preparations, and the passenger sat alone with his thoughts.

My coffin is indeed onboard this plane, human sow. Had I the time, I would make you share it with me. You and your friend should consider yourselves very fortunate that I have other matters to attend to. Perhaps on my return home, I will see fit to turn you. Or I may see fit to render you limb from limb. I will have time aplenty to play with new toys after tonight. There is a wrong to be righted.

The elder vampire named Vladimir closed his eyes and began to rest.

MORNING AFTER

Vicki awoke alone this morning. While she wasn't crazy about that, she completely understood why. It was already daylight, and she knew Marcus had to be out of the sunlight by now. Plus, she had to get to work. Monday mornings were always the busiest time for her. There were already several voice mails on her phone, and she knew they were tips about things happening in the city. She'd get to them soon enough. Right now, Vicki just wanted to lie on her bed for a while and reminisce about everything that happened last night.

Damn, he was GOOD. Oh my God, no man has ever done me the way he did. I don't even know how many times I came. He was so good, so gentle, like he loved me. That's how he made love to me.

Vicki came to learn a lot more about Marcus after the lovemaking. Lying on her bed, she remembered how it was just a few hours earlier. She laid with him, looking into his eyes with his arms around her, listening as he told her more about him and his friends.

"Vladimir sent us to set up a new clan in Paris," Marcus told her. "We skipped France and kept going all the way to America. I believed that Vladimir would not be able to find us over such a large distance. He kept tabs on every member of his clan through mental telepathy, but so far it looks like my hunch was correct. The Atlantic Ocean is too great a distance for even his powers."

"Whose idea was it to even try this?"

"It was mine. For too long, I was tired of hunting humans to drink their blood. It made me sick to do Vladimir's will, but I...all of us....were his slaves. I even contemplated stepping out into the daylight just to end it all. More than once. When Vladimir chose me to start the new clan, I got together several friends whom had grown to feel the same as I did. We told Vlad we would contact him once we got to Paris. I think he's still waiting for that call."

That brought a laugh from Vicki. She liked his dry humor. "It's funny hearing you talk. You don't sound like you were raised in America, but you know the language and the lingo."

"We made a conscious decision to learn English when we got here. We knew we would have to be able to blend in among humans, so we watched American television and studied words we didn't know online. Alexander really picked it up well. He was always sarcastic, so the American way of speaking fits him perfect."

"I'd like to meet your friends," Vicki replied.

"You'd like them. We even have a little nickname; The Lost. Alexander's idea, of course."

Marcus then fell silent, and hugged Vicki tight. Much as she wanted to continue the conversation, laying in his arms felt so comfortable, she quickly fell asleep soon after. Hours later, she awoke to Marcus gone. She had no way to contact him, but she had a feeling that he could find her if he wanted to.

If tomorrow is his last night here, then I'm taking the day off. I want to be there with him. Can I handle that, though? Can I deal with watching him die if that happens? Vicki couldn't answer that question, but she knew she cared for him enough to want to be there with him regardless.

She got out of bed, and while walking to her bathroom she noticed a piece of paper taped to the mirror on her dresser. *He left a note!* Opening the note, she read what was written:

Hello, my love. Sorry for leaving you but I think you know why I had to. Come by and see me and my friends tonight around 8 o'clock. 125 Creston Ave. The Bronx. Top floor. Be warned, the place is a mess. Love, Marcus.

Vicki smiled, and then rushed to the shower. She was going to take care all her job-related stuff today, then hop on the A train to see her man. *I'll be there, baby. I promise you.*

***

Several hours earlier in the South Bronx, the object of her thoughts approached the building he and the others called home. Marcus, a vampire falling in love with a human female, entered through the front entrance of the building and proceeded to walk up the stairs, a strange mixture of elation and sadness whirling inside of him. Elation because soon Marcus and the others would be on their way to the church, and from there hopefully on their way to Heaven. Sadness because he believed tonight was the last time he would see Vicki Ramos.

It has to be this way. I don't know if it'll be possible for us to be together. Certainly, not now. She's alive, I'm an undead freak. If I'm correct, and the salvation at the church is a success, there's a good chance our bodies will turn to dust. How is she supposed to love a lifeless husk? A pile of dead, ashen flesh? Maybe she can scoop me into a bag and take me out to dinner.

Marcus stopped at the top of the stairway and shook his head. Sad as he was, he didn't want to waste his time on what couldn't be. Instead he focused on what had already been. *At least I was able to spend some time with her. I'm thankful for that. Thankful that she could look past my condition and make love to me. I didn't feel undead last night, I felt ALIVE. I know she'll come by tonight. I just want to tell her what I feel. I want to hold her, to feel her, just one more time. Because maybe, just maybe, we can survive tomorrow night.*

Entering the makeshift vampire lair, Marcus walked

over to his coffin and laid himself in it. He closed the lid and drifted to sleep with thoughts of Vicki in his head.

MEET THE VAMPIRES

Fort Apache: The Bronx was the first thing to come to mind.

Vicki Ramos stood in front of 125 Creston Avenue, the address Marcus gave her. It was older apartment building, abandoned and boarded up. Whoever owned it had long since let it slip into ruin. It was the kind of building that represented a New York from several decades ago, when the city was broke and falling into urban decay. It reminded her of the movie *Fort Apache The Bronx*, a film about a New York City police prescient in a rundown section of the Bronx. This was the New York Vicki's parents always talked about. Dirty neighborhoods, the Son of Sam, the blackout of '77, etc. She didn't think there were any more buildings like this left in the city.

Vicki cautiously approached the front door of the building. Though the building was basically condemned, the door swung open with ease. *This is the address he gave me. It better be open.*

***

Marcus could have sworn he heard a knocking at the door.

He was still asleep in his coffin when the sound came to him. He wasn't sure at first because he couldn't remember the last time someone actually knocked on the door. The vampires didn't exactly have a lot of visitors. Then Marcus heard it again, louder this time. It was someone knocking at the door all right, but who…VICKI! It was her! Suddenly, he remembered that he invited her to come over this evening. Marcus threw open his coffin lid and jumped out. He knew it was her right away; he could feel her presence outside.

Marcus rushed to the door and opened it. "Hey stranger," he said.

"I'm so glad you're here," Vicki gushed.

This place gave her the creeps. She was hoping Marcus would open the door quickly, and he did. Now the creeps gave way to happiness and relief. She walked up close, threw her arms around him and kissed him, and Marcus gladly kissed her back. Closing the door behind them, he led her inside.

"Told you it was a mess," he said.

"No doubt. This place could use a woman's touch."

A voice shot out from nowhere. "It DOES have a woman's touch."

Vicki quickly looked to her left, where she saw a teenage girl. It was Mila, leaning against a wall, looking annoyed and not too happy to have company. The young vamp eyed Vicki up and down, not as a meal but as an unwanted visitor. She spoke again. "It has MY touch."

Marcus cleared his throat. "Vicki, this is Mila. Mila, this is my friend Vicki."

Vicki flashed a friendly smile. "Hi. Nice to meet you."

"Hi," Mila responded, trying not to be rude for Marcus's sake. She then walked away towards the living room area, sitting on the sofa. Already in the living room were the other vampires, all seated and all eyes on Vicki.

Marcus led Vicki into the large open area. She saw everyone there. They looked either annoyed or indifferent to her visit. Vicki didn't need to be told that her presence there was not all that welcome.

"Everyone, this is my friend Vicki," Marcus's intro

was met by silence. After a few seconds, Alexander spoke up.

"How thoughtful of you, Marcus. You had dinner delivered tonight. Thanks, I was getting hungry."

"Knock it off, Alex," Marcus snapped, with more than a hint of anger in his voice.

"Why did you bring her here, Marcus?" Gennady asked.

Vicki recognized him as the rude guy at the club the night she found Marcus. There was no mistaking that thick Russian accent. *No wonder Marcus showed up so fast.*

"Right before the most important event of our lives, you bring a stranger into our mist."

"She's not a stranger, not to me. She's a good friend."

"I bet she is," Mila snarked.

Vicki didn't like where this was going. Bad enough when a bunch of people didn't like you; when it's a bunch of vampires, that's not a place anyone wants to be.

"Look, I'm sorry if my coming here is such a problem. I know when I'm not wanted. I'll let myself out. Thanks for the warm welcome." Vicki headed for the door.

Marcus gave a look of anger towards his brethren, then followed Vicki to the outside hallway.

"Sorry to bother your friends," Vicki said. "I shouldn't have come."

"Don't say that. This was my fault. I didn't tell them you were coming, and I should have. I didn't take their feelings into consideration. I'm the one who should be sorry"

"I don't wanna leave you, but I don't wanna make your friends upset either."

"It's OK. We'll go somewhere else, maybe to Central Park or-"

"Excuse me miss." It was Stephen. Standing behind Marcus, the newest vampire to the clan spoke to Vicki. "Don't be upset. My friends may have been rude, but you got to understand what we've all been going through and what we're about to through tomorrow night. Everyone's nervous and on edge. We just weren't expecting company, and to be honest seeing you reminds all of us what we lost, and what we're trying to get back. And yeah Marcus, it's your fault." Stephen smiled, and Marcus smiled back. "Please come back inside. If you're a friend of Marcus, that's good enough for me."

Vicki was touched. Marcus had good taste in friends. "Thank you. I'd be happy to come in."

The three of them walked back inside to the living room area. Vicki sat down next to Mila, who seemed a bit friendlier this time. At least she wasn't outright hostile. Marcus and Stephen hung near Alexander, and soon all three were in conversation. Gennady sat in the corner of the area by himself and appeared to want it that way.

Vicki broke the ice with Mila. "I like how you did your hair."

Mila cracked a slight smile. Her hair was pulled into two small pigtails, streaked with hot pink colors and tied with little dead flowers at the end. "Thanks. I like trying different looks. It gets guy's attention whenever I go clubbing. Free drinks, you know."

"That's the best things about clubbing. The free alcohol is worth all the bad one-liners."

"Most of the time. I've heard some real bad ones."

Vicki and Mila continued to talk. Marcus noticed this and was happy to see it. Despite the frosty introduction, both ladies had hit it off well. He said to Stephen: "Thanks for what you did, Stephen. I appreciate it."

"No problem, Marcus. I know how she feels. It wasn't that long ago that I was in her shoes. That's why I came here with you. I want to get back to that."

"We all do, Stephen. We all do."

Alexander spoke. "Me too, although I gotta admit I will miss some things about being a vampire. The power we have, the things we can do, it's pretty damn intoxicating. Man, if I could be human and keep these powers, that'd be perfect."

Gennady walked up to join them. He heard what Alexander said. "It would be hard to give up these powers. Too hard. I'm having second thoughts, Marcus. I'm not sure

I'll be joining you all tomorrow night."

Marcus was floored. "What are you talking about? Gennady, you can't be serious. You were one of the first ones I came to with this idea. What's wrong?"

"Nothing. It's just…I don't feel like I belong in this world. I've never felt comfortable during these modern times. I want to go back to my time, to the life I had before, and that's not possible. Why go back to being human and giving up these powers for a world I want no part of?"

"That's assuming we even survive this, big guy," replied Alexander. "Don't tell me you're not tired of being a vampire. The powers are cool and everything, but I'd really like to go back to eating real food and loving a real woman."

None of them noticed Vicki and Mila leave for the door together. They walked outside and closed the door behind them, while Marcus continued to plead with Gennady.

"Gen, it's OK to be nervous. You're not alone, no matter what you think. Come on, you were the one who kept me going through this whole ordeal. I would've killed myself a long time ago if it wasn't for you telling me to never give up hope. You're the reason I'm here right now."

Marcus placed his hand on Gennady's arm. "You're not alone, you hear me? You never will be so long as we're still here. I'd never make you do something you wouldn't want to do, so whatever you decide I'll respect that. But I'd really want you to be there with us tomorrow. I need you. I need all of you guys. I can't go back to being human all by myself."

Alexander leaned into Gennady's ear. "If you come with us, I'll take you to a strip club when we're done. Lap dances and champagne room are my treat." Gennady and the others laughed.

While the group was talking, Mila and Vicki were outside in the hallway, standing by the window. Mila was puffing on a cigarette, while Vicki was checking out Mila and wondering just how young she was. They had been talking for a little while already.

"You love him, don't you?" Mila asked.

"Yeah. I think I do. Crazy, huh? Not just that I'm falling for him so fast, but…technically he's not actually alive. But there's a good person in there, a good soul, and that's what I love about him. Well, there's also the way he used his tongue."

"Ha! Yeah, I can imagine. I can't wait to have sex. Real, human sex, I'm dying for it! I was turned right after my 16th birthday, still a virgin. Every time I try to hook up with a guy at a club, the dudes here get involved. Like hello, I'm a vampire! I can handle myself if a guy gets too rough, ya know? Sheesh, I gotta come out here just to enjoy a smoke."

"I'm so glad I'm an only child. Older brothers can mess up your game big time. But you can't blame them. They're just trying to protect you. You're still a baby to them."

"Yeah, I guess so. It's cool. I do feel safe around them. Ya know, I like hanging with you. It's nice having another female to talk to. I'm glad Marcus brought you over. I mean, I wasn't happy about it at first, but I'm glad now."

"Thanks! I'm glad too."

Both girls were enjoying their conversation, so much so that they paid no attention to the floor of the hallway. Normally, ignoring the hallway floor would be no cause for concern. Except that at that moment, something was there the girls did not see at all. Something that was slowly creeping toward them.

A thick, foggy mist.

***

Ahhhh, yes. There you are. I can feel you now.
This time, there is no mistake.
This time I know exactly where you are.
It has taken many months to find you. No longer will the ocean hide you from me. Take pleasure in the gifts I have sent you, Marcus. I take pleasure in knowing you will watch

my spies tear apart your traitorous followers. What will you tell them, swine? When they are dying in agony, will you apologize for daring to lead them away from me?

I trusted you to build a new clan, to expand our horde and ensure our continued existence. You were to go to Paris. You were to make contact as soon as you found a secure resting place. You did neither, Marcus. Instead you led them here to America. The only time I had ever entrusted an underling to go forth without the supervision of the clan, the one time I had ever placed my trust in someone other than myself, and the end result was your goddamn betrayal.

Damn you Marcus, why?! What was your reason for defying me? You will tell me. I prayed to the unholy father that you and your fellow traitors would still be in existence when I found you, and to my delight you are. I can feel your brainwaves; I can sense where you are to be this night. Rest assured, you wasted mass of dead human flesh, I WILL BE THERE AS WELL.

AMBUSH

Vladimir was here, and Marcus knew it right away.

It was hard to explain. Talking with Gennady, Stephen and Alexander, Marcus was relaxed and feeling hopeful about their future. He noticed Vicki and Mila were no longer on the sofa, but he could sense that they were fine outside. *Good. They're getting along. I knew they would once they got to know each other.* Their awkwardness in the beginning seemed to be gone. Everything was fine.

Suddenly he felt it, like a spike to the heart. A stirring in his dead soul, long forgotten yet still familiar. He could feel Vladimir's presence. There was no mistaking it. Somehow, someway, the elder had found them. He was somewhere in the city. Marcus had barely processed that information...his first thought was to warn the others and prepare for a defense...when another terrible feeling came to him.

Vicki and Mila were under attack.

"NO!!" Marcus screamed. The girls were still in the hallway, still close enough for him to save them. He rushed to the door, hoping we would get there quick enough. Vicki was still alive, and she was right outside, and we would be right there... -

BOOM!

The front door exploded inward, knocking Marcus to the floor. Shaking his head, lying on the floor, Marcus looked up and saw four figures in the doorway. He knew right away who they were; Vladimir's spies. The minions who had always followed Vlad close by, ready to serve his whim at a moment's notice. So frightening were they that even fellow vampires in the clan knew to stay clear of them. Looking more like demons than humans, the spies all possessed curved razor sharp nails, long fangs, sunken red eyes, and a penchant for violence. They were spawns of the Devil himself, and they were right here right now, ready to kill everyone in sight. Including the woman Marcus was falling in love with.

The creature in the front walked over to Marcus and attempted to grin.

"Vladimir gives his greetings, worm."

***

Vicki was the first one to notice the mist.

She was having a good time talking with Mila. Vicki came to find that Mila, although shy and curt when they first met, was quite the chatterbox when she opened up. The ladies discussed topics like sex, vampires, love and clubbing. Vicki liked her and the feeling was mutual for Mila as well. Vicki was about to start singing the praises of marijuana (*Can a vampire get high?*) when she saw the mist in the hallway. The last times she saw the mist, it was at the docks and the alley where she was saved by Marcus. The mist meant vampires were coming. But she was already with the vampires, so...

"Mila, please tell me that mist has something to do with you."

"Huh?" Mila looked at Vicki with a quizzical look on her face. *What mist was she talking about? The mist only comes up as protection when we're on the hunt.* Mila turned her head towards the hallway and saw the mist as well. She knew right away what this meant. They were under attack.

"Get behind me!" Mila screamed at Vicki.

The young vampire jumped in front of her and crouched into a defensive position. Her fangs bared, her nails ready to render, Mila no longer looked like a teenage girl but more like a fierce jungle cat ready to pounce. Whatever was here posed a threat to her new friend, and she was not going to let anything happen to her. Mila hissed out her words towards the mist in a gritty, feral voice. "Leave us alone, you bastards!"

Vicki was frightened as hell. She figured out pretty quickly that this was vampires attacking them. But who? Mila seemed to know. Maybe the vampire Marcus told her about had found them. Mila was the only thing standing between Vicki and certain death. She opened her mouth to scream for her protector, and that's when the attack came.

A demonic vampire spy jumped out of the mist. Flashing long fangs and knife-like claws, the creature crashed into Mila. Vicki moved out of the way just in time as both vampires slammed into the wall near the window. The spy savagely clawed and tore at Mila. Intent on ripping her to shreds, starting with her neck. Mila knew she was in a fight for her life. She had never been hit so hard. The young vamp fought back, kicking the demon in the gut and throwing him off of her. It crashed into the side wall and popped right back up, again pouncing on Mila.

"Vicki run! Get out of here!"

Vicki ran down the hallway, towards the door leading to Marcus' apartment. At that moment, she wanted more than anything to get to safety, to get to Marcus, to tell the others that Mila was under attack so they could save her, and to get the hell away from the monster in the mist. As she got closer to the door, she could see that it had been blasted open. Pieces of the door littered the hallway floor. Had this creature already attacked Marcus and the others?

Before she could think any further, a large weight jumped on her back. Vicki's body slammed to the floor. Though she was dazed and in pain, she was aware enough to know what had landed on her, and awake enough to feel the thing turn her body around and expose her neck. Vicki saw the blood red eyes of this hell spawn and felt it's hot, fetid breath upon her.

Despite her fear, Vicki wasn't going down without a fight. She reared back her right hand and punched the creature in the face with everything she had. The thing's face felt like hard leather. *Like a cheap purse you buy on Canal Street.* More angry than stunned by her punch, the vampire spy opened its maw and prepared to feast on Vicki's throat, but it was not to be.

Mila was in pain, a sensation she hadn't felt since she was human. But she was also enraged like she had never been before, and she possessed powers to do something with that rage. Running up to the monster, she grabbed it from behind, pulled it away from Vicki, and with all her strength flipped the monster over her head and smashed it through the hallway floor to the next story below.

Mila stood looking down through the large hole she just created, as if admiring her handiwork. She turned to look at Vicki and nodded. Vicki nodded back.

"I owe you one, *meija*," she said.

Mila smiled at her. Breathing hard breaths, her dead skin bloodied and bruised, the young girl looked like a fierce warrior. It was as if Mila had grown up 10 years in the last few minutes, and in a way she had. "Get me into your friend's club and we'll call it even."

The good feeling did not last long. With a terrible scream, the demon vampire exploded through the floor. Mila fell to the floor, and before she could get her bearings the beast was upon her.

Vicki could only watch as the young girl tried to withstand the creature's vicious onslaught. It fought with a berserker fury, tearing away at Mila's flesh. Still reeling from her earlier encounter but determined not to let her friend die, Vicki crawled toward Marcus's door. He HAD to still be alive.

Please baby, I need you. Mila's dying! Please Marcus, save us!

***

Inside the apartment, it was a battle royal.

Marcus was initially stunned by the exploding entrance of Vladimir's minions but it did not take long for him to recover. He had no choice, really. The entire group ran into the lair intent on murder and mayhem. There were four of them, all the same in appearance, and they targeted Gennady, Stephen and Alexander. The first creature, the one who gave Marcus such a warm greeting, jumped on him and held him to the ground. Marcus could see his friends fighting for their (undead) lives against this pack of bloodthirsty killers. A cold hand grasped his neck, and the creature leaned in towards his face.

"Not yet for you," it whispered in Marcus' ear. "Our lord wants you for himself. For now, you can watch your fellow traitors die."

Sending his slaves to do the dirty work so he can sweep in and deal the final blow. That's Vladimir all right, and quite frankly Marcus was goddamn tired of it all. He never asked for this existence, he never asked to be sent to Paris, and now because he and his friends wanted control over their own destiny, they faced extermination.

Marcus was beyond angry; he wanted to give Vlad and his bloodsuckers a good taste of what they had done to others. This cackling fool holding him down would be the first to get that taste.

"The only death I'm going to watch is yours," Marcus growled. Utilizing strength that surprised even himself, Marcus plunged his right hand deep into the creature's chest and ripped out its heart. Blood and tendrils from the demon's chest rained down on him. Surprise would be a good word to describe what the beast felt. Fear would be a good word for what it felt next, as whatever unholy force it possessed evaporated. It fell to the floor with a loud thud and a confused look frozen on its face.

Marcus wasn't done. Rising to his full height and turning his attention to the others, Marcus smiled...but it was not a smile of merriment. This was a smile born of vengeance, of malice; a smile belonging to someone about to embark on a much desired bloody rampage. For 200 years, he had hunted and killed humans, always against his will. For 200 years, he fought against the predatory instinct foisted upon him by the vampire curse. In all of that time, Marcus had never given in to the full bloodthirsty desire roiling within him.

For 200 years….and not one second more. Tonight, in this moment, he would finally give in to the darkest part of him. Marcus would no longer fight the dark power which controlled him. He would open his arms and *welcome* it.

He charged at the other vampire spies attacking his friends. Marcus was in full-bore vampire mode now, and for the first time ever...he was going to *enjoy* it.

***

In the hallway, Vicki kept crawling towards the front door of the apartment. Her head was still spinning and now she could really feel the painful bruises from when she was knocked to the floor. Seconds before she attempted to stand run but fell back to the floor. The attack had taken more from her than she realized. Vicki tried not to pay attention to the sounds of Mila and the monster fighting to the death. Vlad's pit-bull was winning this fight. It threw Mila into the wall, then smashed her on the other wall. She put up a brave fight and refused to give up, but the beatings had taken their toll.

Barely conscious, Mila could do no more and collapsed to the ground. Her breath came in labored spurts. The beast stood over her beaten body, and with a hyena-like laugh, picked up Mila by her throat. It turned its head to look at Vicki, a predatory stare. Vicki knew that after it was done with Mila, she would be next, and she didn't know if she would reach the door in time.

Maybe the creature was overconfident. Maybe it believed the vampire girl in his grip was finished. Whatever the case was, taking its eyes off of his prey was a fatal mistake. Mila's eyes suddenly opened, and with her last burst of energy, she plunged her nails into the thing's neck, and pushed them both off the wall. Despite the monster still gripping her throat, Mila was strong enough to steer it where she wanted it to go. She was going to kill this thing even at the cost of her life. Mila screamed out in defiance.

"Go to fucking hell, and this time stay there!"

Picking up speed, Mila drove the demon with a final thrust...through the gaping hole in the floor. Both figures disappeared from view, followed two seconds later by a loud bang and horrific screams. All of this happened right in front of a startled Vicki.

"Mila!" she yelled. There was no mistaking the sounds of two voices screaming, no mistaking a high-pitched female voice. Vicki peered down the hole. She knew what she saw, but she refused to believe it. She didn't want to believe it.

Summoning her strength, Vicki stood up and lumbered down the stairway to the floor below. There, at the end of the stairs, lay the bodies of Mila and the demon. The young vamp lay on top of her attacker, face to face. With her last effort, she did manage to finally kill the monster by impaling it on a large wooden plank jutting from the floor. The plank tore through the heart of the creature...and through Mila's heart as well. A sharp piece of wood stuck out from Mila's back, covered in blood.

Vicki knelt down close to her friend. "Mila," she whispered. "Come on girl, talk to me."

Mila was not done yet. She slowly raised her head to look at Vicki and cracked a smile. She defeated a demon from hell and saved her new friend Vicki. Mila felt so proud about that. Her smile gave way to anguish, as the death throes rattled her little frame.

She wanted to do so much with her new life, this young girl turned vampire. She believed that Marcus' plan would work, that she would come back as a regular teen-age girl. Mila wanted to find love, to be loved, to make peace with God, but it was not to be. There would be no salvation, no trip to church. There would be nothing.

Her eyes met Vicki's, both filled with tears. Vicki held Mila's hand and squeezed, perhaps hoping to transfer some life to her. Mila wanted to say something. She wanted to say good-bye. She wanted to tell Vicki thanks for being here for her in these last moments so she wouldn't be alone. But no words came. The light in her eyes vanished. Her head slumped forward. The end for her was here. Mila, the teen girl vampire who hoped to regain her humanity, died.

There was nothing more Vicki could do. She laid her head on her friend's shoulder, and wept. It wasn't long before she heard a comforting voice.

"Are you OK?"

Seconds earlier, Marcus burst into the hallway, searching for Vicki. He cursed himself for giving in to his bloodlust and his thirst for revenge. He should have been out here saving Vicki and Mila. If he lost her because of this, he'd never forgive himself. He sensed her, though. She was downstairs, and Mila was with her. Running downstairs, Marcus found them both. Only one was alive.

Vicki felt relief and sadness seeing Marcus, and she hugged him tightly. At least HE was still alive. "She's gone," Vicki sobbed. "Marcus, she saved my life and I couldn't do anything to save her."

Marcus already knew. He sensed her life-force was gone. Mila's spirit had left her body.

Vicki sobbed in his arms, while he tried to comfort her as best he could. "There was nothing you could've done, honey. I should have been protecting both of you."

Kneeling down Marcus reached for Mila's face. Gently, he closed her eyes. Despite the blood and bruises on her, she looked at peace. Marcus was so proud of her. She held her own against one of Vlad's spies. He always knew she had more to her than anyone, even Mila herself, imagined. *She was just a child. Mila, I'm so sorry. I failed to protect you. Please forgive me.*

"Is everyone else OK?" Vicki asked.

"Yeah. They're hurting but still alive...well, as alive as

we can be."

"What happened? What was that thing?"

"Things. Several of them busted into the apartment and attacked us."

"You mean there was more than one?"

"Yeah. We can't stay here. We've got to go."

***

Arthur Murray wasn't used to getting phone calls at this time, several minutes pass ten o'clock at night. He had been sitting in his living room, going over notes for weekly sermons, when the call came. The ringing made him jump. Arthur had no idea who it could be...wait a minute. He DID have an idea, and that concerned him.

"Hello?"

"Father, it's Marcus."

"Good evening, Marcus. I wasn't expecting to hear from you tonight."

"I need your help. We can't wait till tomorrow. We need the church tonight. Please help us."

***

It's so quiet here.

Where's everybody at? Vicki was right here. We were talking in the hallway and -

Oh yeah, I forgot. I'm dead. Shit.

Still should be proud of myself though. I killed that demon, took him on and took him out! Really wish I hadn't killed myself too.

So this is the afterlife? Whoopee-fucking-doo. I mean, it's better than burning in flames and stuff. No red guy with horns and a pitchfork here. Ha! Marcus used to tell me that he looks a little different than that, but I don't care. He's still a doofus in a dumb red outfit to me.

Hey, my bruises are gone! And I'm not bleeding. That's

a start. Hole in my chest? That's gone too. YES!!! But now what? I hope this ain't Heaven either. There's nothing and no one here. Just a lotta light. Maybe it's a Heaven waiting room or something. Like the clubs in New York.

Damn I really wanted to go to that new club Vicki's friend was opening. Sounded wicked as hell. Fucking Vladimir! I hope Marcus sticks a giant cross up your ass, bitch! I'm not scared of you anymore. I just took out one of your boys! I'm not scared of anything. Not even death.

OK maybe death, just a little, if it's gonna stay this way. Being alone sucks.

Whoa, maybe this means I still got a shot at going to Heaven! Like, I'm supposed to be in hell now, right? So if I'm not, then maybe...shit, I don't even wanna think about it. If I'm wrong, I'm gonna start freaking out and start crying and shit. Like a baby.

It's so quiet here, for real. So, so quiet...
Hey, wait a minute! Am I riding in a car?

***

Alexander didn't want to steal the car, but they really had no choice.

The attack at their lair had left the group battered physically and desperate mentally. Marcus told them that Vladimir was here in New York City, and it wasn't hard to figure out why. He was going to kill them all. Forget bringing them back home; the encounter with his band of assassins proved that he was out for blood, and not the drinking kind either. This was their last shot at redemption, their only shot. It had to be tonight, before the elder could find them.

Luckily, Father Murray came through for them. He agreed to set up the church tonight with very little notice. Marcus had no idea what he would've done if the priest hadn't been able to accommodate them so quickly, but that little tidbit he kept to himself. Now all they had to do was hop on the train to mid-town and they'd be set; except that no one wanted to leave Mila's body behind. The others were distraught at the sight of her body impaled at the foot of the stairs, especially Alexander. He was always messing with Mila, and genuinely doubted her ability to handle a serious situation without the guidance of the other vampires. *I'm so glad I was wrong, little sister. You did great.*

All this time Vicki had not left Mila's side. She sat next to her body, still holding her hand. She no longer felt pain or fear, but anger. Her new friend died to protect her. Vicki felt she owed Mila, and the only way she could repay her now was to still try and save her soul. No way Vicki was gonna leave her here to rot. One way or another, Mila was going to the church.

"We can't leave her here, Marcus. We gotta get her to the church. Maybe her soul can still be saved."

"Damn right, she's not staying here," Stephen agreed. "We came here together, we leave here together."

"Train is out of the question," replied Marcus. "So's a taxi. We need a car."

"Too bad the dealership is closed," quipped Alexander. "I'm sure we could get a bloodsucker discount."

"We're gonna make our own discount," said Marcus. "Alex, I need you to steal a car."

"Isn't that a sin? God mentioned it in the Ten Commandments. I don't wanna piss him off before we ask him for eternal salvation, you know?"

"I think he'll understand."

***

Ten minutes later, the entire group rode in a stolen Monte Carlo. Marcus drove with Stephen in the front, while the others sat in the back. Sandwiched between Alexander and Gennady and wearing a long coat, Vicki held Mila in her lap. She was cleaning up her face during the drive, wiping off blood and dirt and trying her best to make her hair look halfway decent. No way was she going to let Mila cross over to the other side looking like a hot mess, Vicki thought. Marcus drove as fast as he could without drawing attention. The last thing they needed was to get pulled over by a cop.

Guilt ate away at Marcus as he drove. Not only did he feel guilty for not being able to protect Vicki and Mila, but he was also beginning to once again doubt this whole ordeal. Ever since they made their break from the clan, Marcus held fast to his convictions and his belief that they could accomplish the impossible. He truly, earnestly believed they could be saved, and it was this unwavering confidence in this idea that also inspired the others. They believed in this plan so strongly because HE believed in it, and they were willing to follow this all the way through to see it happen. When he started to first have his doubts, Vicki showed up in life; Marcus took that as a sign from God to keep going. Now it seemed as though everything was falling apart at once. After 18 months of careful planning and anticipation, right when they were at the doorstep of their goal, it was in jeopardy of failing.

Damn you Vladimir, you just couldn't let go, could you? Five vampires from among a hundred, and you just had to come after us. It's all about control for you. It always has been. You want your little kingdom and you want us all under your thumb. You're not going to ruin this. Not for me, not for any of us. I bet you thought your lapdogs would make this easy for you, huh? I remembered what I can do, and I made sure your buddies knew that. Try to stop us Vlad, and I'll make sure you know it too.

Vicki kept her eyes on Marcus. She could see the worry on his face from the rear view mirror, and she correctly guessed what it was he was thinking about. *Don't you dare blame yourself, Marcus. You've done everything you can do.* She placed her hand on the back of his head and softly caressed his hair. It seemed to relax Marcus a bit, and Vicki could feel some of the tension leave him.

"It's Ok, baby," she said, in the same voice she used to lure him to her bedroom. "Have faith. You got us, and you got me."

Marcus looked at Vicki in the rear view mirror. He smiled, and she smiled back. This must be love, he thought to himself, because just seeing her smile made him feel better. Made him feel that there was still hope. Like he used to feel 200 years ago when he looked into the eyes of the only other woman he ever loved.

"We're gonna be OK," he told Vicki. "I could take you home if you – "

"Don't even play me like that," Vicki scowled. "I didn't just go through all the shit I went through so you could take me home. I got jumped by a vampire thing from hell, OK?! I didn't just deal with that so I could turn around and leave you. I told you I wanted to be there with you when you go to the church, and I'm not gonna put you out there like that. I don't know what I'm getting myself into, but I KNOW what I'm getting myself into."

Marcus gave Vicki a confused look. Even the guys in the back of the car looked confused. "Huh?"

Slightly embarrassed, Vicki waved her hand. "You know what I mean."

"Good," said Alexander. "That makes one of us."

***

Very funny, Alex. Fucking comedian.

What the hell AM I getting myself into? Vampires, monsters, old guys from Europe, and me stuck in the middle. What am I doing here? Don't ask Vicki, you know exactly why. This man...I can't even consider him a vampire...I think I love him. Here he is ready to face the biggest challenge of his life, and he's worried about my safety.

I'm scared. I'm scared as hell. But here I am. You stood by me, so now I got your back, papi.

***

"How far is the church" she asked.

"Not too far," Marcus replied. "We're about 15 minutes away. Father Murray should already be there."

"Remind me to thank him for this," said Gennady. "We owe him more than he can know."

"We're all going to thank him. Not just for helping us out, but for also being our friend."

***

Thank you. Marcus.

Thank you for giving me the information I required. You passed your test with flying colors. I needed a fair assessment of your powers and your anger, and lo you did not disappoint. You displayed all the attributes I saw in you from the beginning. I can feel your anger! I could feel the rage swelling in your chest and the bloodlust consuming you. A pity I was not there to witness you finally succumb to your true calling, but there will be another opportunity coming soon enough. I will see to that.

I have reached my destination.

***

Late Monday night, and the St. Augustine Catholic Church stood closed to all. Except for vampires in search of salvation. Father Murray was almost done preparing for Marcus and his friends, prepping the church for a very special mass. The Bible lay upon the pulpit facing the rows of seats. Bottles of newly blessed holy water placed on a table nearby. A man of God kept busy making sure everything was in place. Not bad considering he had arrived at the church just 25 minutes earlier. Father Murray had never set up a service this quickly but he managed it well nonetheless.

The priest stood at the front of the row of seats, next to the pulpit. For the moment, he was done.

"They should be here anytime now." He often spoke

to himself as he prepared the church for mass, and he was especially excited about the mass tonight. Excited, and frightened as hell.

Father Murray knew he would be facing a huge challenge this night. He was attempting to accomplish a task that had never been done before, as far as he knew. Now it had to be done earlier than planned.

Arthur was dealing with a clear sense of anxiety. This couldn't be helped, that element of unpredictability was expected to be there, but what had really scared the good pastor was a base fear, a little knot in his stomach telling him that something was going to happen tonight. Whether that something was good or bad the priest could not tell, and that was what worried him.

What happened to Marcus to make him ask for the church service tonight, right now? The priest didn't press him for an explanation. He figured he'd find out eventually. But if it was bad enough to force Marcus to change his plans, then it was most likely some very bad news.

The old priest took a deep breath. Part of him wanted to cancel this whole thing, to go home and call it a night, but Father Murray had made a promise to God and to Marcus. A promise made is a promise kept, especially so for a man of the cloth.

And can you imagine what would happen if the vampire wanted revenge on you for skipping out? You might be safe hiding inside the church, or you might not. Care to put that little myth to the test, Arthur old boy?

Not really, he answered himself.

With that thought fading away from his mind, Father Murray walked down the hall towards the front door of the church. Reaching for the door handle, he noticed the door was already open, almost closed but slightly ajar. There appeared to be a figure standing just outside the door, dressed in a long, dark trench coat, and the figure stood silently as if waiting for an invitation to come inside. Unable to make out a face, and believing the figure to be who he thought it was, Father

Murray opened the door and uttered the last words he would ever speak.

"Marcus, is that you?"

DESTINATION

Weaving through the Manhattan traffic was as stressful as Vicki thought it would be. At one point, a police cruiser pulled up behind them. Marcus told everyone to stay calm and act natural, and Vicki prayed that they wouldn't get pulled over. Suddenly, the cruiser's lights flashed on, and the cop peeled off to another destination at high speed. Everyone in the car exhaled.

Minutes later, the group reached the church. Marcus pulled the car unto the small driveway right next to the church and parked. He tried to extend his mental reach to see if he could sense Father Murray (and Vlad too, come to think of it.) Nothing was there, nothing concrete. Marcus didn't like that. He should have been able to feel something. He usually did when the pastor was nearby. Now there was nothing. Maybe the close proximity to the church was affecting him. It could be his nerves, or it could be Vladimir.

Heh. A nervous vampire. I should write a book if I survive this.

The others piled out of the car and took their steps to the front of the church where Marcus stood. Alexander was carrying Mila, who looked like a sleeping child in his arms. Vicki held Marcus's hand and stood close to him. One by one, the group all looked at each other. For a minute, no word was said. Their eyes told the story well enough. All the planning, the running, the long exodus across the ocean to reach America, everything they had sacrificed, all lead to this moment. Marcus was not alone in his nervousness; everyone was on the same page.

Alexander finally spoke. "Well guys and gals, this is it."

Marcus looked at his fellow vampires. "Everybody ready?" They all nodded in agreement.

Marcus looked at Vicki, then kissed her on her lips. "I can't tell you how much it means to me that you're here. Thank you"

Vicki gently touched his face. "You're gonna be OK. We're all gonna be OK."

Marcus then gazed upon the church doors, took a deep breath, and steeled his resolve. "It's time."

Marcus paused for the slightest second. Then, with a casual effort, he lifted his right leg and placed his foot on the first step. Vickie moved with him, following his every move. Immediately afterward, Alexander did the same. Then Gennady. Then Stephen. The group moved as one, walking up the stairs to the church front door

All the vampires felt a sense of relief. Gennady in particular, who only a short while earlier had expressed his doubts about becoming human, felt waves of peace come over him. He too, had gone centuries without experiencing these feelings. He had his doubts about whether his friend's plans would come to fruition. Now those doubts and fears were gone. Gennady had placed his trust and faith in Marcus, and now he was merely several steps away from being rewarded for that faith.

Stephen, on the other hand, never doubted his friend. In just a short time as a member of the vampire clan, he had seen how vicious Vladimir could be. None of the other vampires dared to cross him, or fail to obey his orders. Marcus' plan to run away to America took more courage and commitment then he had ever seen from either a human or a vampire. Desperate as he was to retrieve his humanity,

Stephen was willing to follow Marcus to hell and back. With each step he took, he came closer to the end of his hope's journey.

Alexander took his own steps to the church door. Holding Mila's body close to him, coming ever closer to whatever lay ahead, redemption or damnation. There were certain things about being a vampire that he was going to miss, no doubt. Physical abilities much greater than any mortal. The way he and the others would become one with the mist, flowing along with its currents until their prey was in site. *Damn, that was so much fun. But I'd rather have my humanity back.*

Mila's head rested on his shoulder. She looked so beautiful, so at peace. She looked almost fully human. Were her bruises healing? And was…was that a smile on face? As he reached the top step, Alexander lowered his head slightly, and kissed the beautiful young creature on her forehead. He whispered in her ear. Something about regret and forgiveness. And love.

Marcus finally stood in front of the church door. He was not alone.

The woman he loved and his friends stood with him. A unified front. The time for hesitation was done. No more reflecting on the past, no more wrestling with self-doubt and trepidation. The time was now. The door to their future stood mere inches from him. Without delay, Marcus grabbed the door handle, pushed it open, and stepped inside the church.

He expected something to happen. Anything. Burning fire, a bright light, loud trumpets blaring…some kind of reaction. But there was nothing. It was all candlelight and silence. The group didn't know if that meant they should feel relieved or concerned.

Marcus walked further into the church. He had an idea of what the inside of a church looked like from dozens of pictures he had seen, and in here it looked exactly like he thought it would. Two large rows of seats were separated by a long walkway leading to a pulpit in front of a large stage.

Statues and paintings of Jesus Christ and other religious figures adorned the walls. Candles lit the spacious interior, casting shadows of the others as they entered the church.

Peaceful. Serene. Everything he had been told Heaven was. This…THIS…must be what salvation feels like.

Except…Father Murray was not here.

"Where's the priest". Alexander wondered, not the only one thinking that question.

"Maybe he's in the back," Marcus replied. "Father Murray! It's me, Marcus. I'm here with my friends. Are you here?"

Marcus would get his answer. Not in the form of Arthur Murray's friendly voice, but in the form of his lifeless body falling from the ceiling and landing with a loud thud on the walkway.

The priest's broken form lay awkwardly on the church floor. There was no doubt of his condition; his legs were broken and bent at unnatural angles, his arms sprawled flat, and most disturbing of all, his head had been turned completely around. He now faced backwards, a look of horror was etched forever on his face. This was the sad proof that this friendly man of God, this man who had volunteered to try to save the souls of a group of bloodsuckers he had never met, had died a most horrible and frightening death.

A loud scream rose from Vicki's throat. She was prepared for anything, they all were prepared, but not for this. They were expecting to see him a living, smiling man welcoming them into his church, a friendly man of God whom had promised to help them. This was not to be.

"NOOOOO!!!!!" Marcus could only scream this word. He quickly bent down close to his friend. In vain, he sought for some way for him to be alive, though he knew it could not be. For a horrific moment, Marcus looked over the body of his friend, while the screams and rumblings from his fellow vampires hung in the background. Looking closer on Arthur's throat, Marcus saw two small puncture wounds, caked with dried blood. This left no doubt as to the author of this murder.

Marcus knew. They all knew.
HE was here.

CONFRONTATION (2)

How dare you, Marcus. How DARE you cry tears for this worthless human. He is nothing more than food, yet you cry for him. I cannot begin to fathom how much your actions disgust me.

It is now clear to me; you were never worthy of the gifts I bestowed upon you. I wanted you to rule along my side. To expand on what I created. Curse your fucking dead soul, Marcus!! You have made me question my own judgement!

I will wait no longer. You and your fellow traitors will face your punishment. You will all face me. NOW.

***

From on high, the shadow came. A large ocean of darkness appeared above the group. A vast black expanse covering the roof. The fire from the candles flickered and bent against the dark power, some going out completely.

The vampires knew what this was. They knew WHO it was.

Oh God, that must be him. That's Vladimir, Vicki thought. *Jesus Christ, protect us. Santa Maria, Madre de Dios...*

Alexander turned to Vicki and placed Mila into her arms. "Take her and go. You can't be here."

"I can't leave Marcus! I promised him…"

Marcus quickly turned to Vicki. "You have to go, my love." He quickly kissed her forehead…a moment which felt like forever…then looked into her eyes. "Go."

Staring into her lover's eyes, holding back tears, Vicki nodded. This was no time to argue. She would see him again, this she believed. But right now she had to go.

Vicki moved fast toward the church doors. Carrying Mila's limp body, she kicked at the front door, forcing it open. No sooner did she step outside when the doors slammed violently shut behind her. Suddenly it was quiet. Vicki looked back in horror. Whatever was going to happen, it was going to be between the vampires inside. No human would be a part of it.

Vicki quickly walked to the side of the church, to avoid being seen by anyone on the street. Once there, a million thoughts raced through Vicki's mind. Should she hide Mila's body and leave? Should she try to get back inside and face certain death? Should she call the cops? What about another church?

For the first time in her adult life, Vicki Ramos was frozen with doubt. She did not know what to do. Scared and confused, Vicki looked at Mila. The beautiful young vampire was silent, forever to sleep. In her desperation, she called to her friend for help.

"Mila, I don't know what to do. I don't… I don't know…"

Yes, you do.

What? Those three words echoed in her mind. She heard them, but they didn't come from anywhere else but inside her head.

You love him, right? Then you know what to do. Girl, you've always known. I know you're scared but you got this. OK? YOU GOT THIS. Just hide me in the bushes next to the church and go do your thing.

You know what to do, Vicki. Marcus made sure of it. YOU KNOW.

In an instant, everything became clear in Vicki's mind. Suddenly, she DID know. The doubt was gone, replaced by the usual Vicki Ramos focus and determination.

Vicki wasted no time. She placed Mila's body underneath a row of bushes located to the side of the church building. Before she left, she hugged Mila tight.

"Thanks, Mila. May God bless you and bring you home to Heaven."

The Puerto Rican mami from the Bronx then stood tall, turning to face the church where the love of her life faced an enemy of unspeakable evil and power.

"I'm coming, baby. I got this."

NOW

The shadow on the roof of the church came down slowly, like a curtain closing at the end of a stage show. It enveloped the entire church in darkness as it descended. The remaining lit candles barely held their flame as darkness fell, powerless against this dreaded evil. Moving closer to the floor, the shadow slowly gave way to the form of a creature of the night, a spawn of the devil himself thousands of years old. The form of Vladimir touched the floor.

The group could only stand and watch, feelings of loss and anger and hopelessness shared between them. All of them had such high hopes for tonight. Despite the attack on their home, despite the loss of dear Mila, they still remained positive their dream would be realized. At the very least an honest attempt to make it so. Now all that was left was to face their almost imminent demise at the hands of an Elder.

For a few seconds, no one moved. Silence as both Elder and vampires faced each other. Dressed in an all-black suit, the lingering sulfur swirling around him, the demon stood several feet from the others. Little choice they had but to look upon Vladimir's face; a withering sack of alabaster white skin pulled taut by centuries of use, housing blood red eyes and thin cracked lips.

Vladimir stared at the group, making sure to look each one in the eye. He saved the longest hardest stare for his former prize pupil. The one who had taken his gifts and departed, who had dared to befriend the food as if it were worthy of anything other than fodder.

Deep, deep down in the dead black heart of this elder, there was the slightest, the smallest, most minimal strain of what could be called hurt feelings.

"Marcus," it grated, a voice dripping with disdain and contempt. Vladimir barely sounded human, and he made no attempt to hide what he was thinking.

"Vladimir," Marcus replied.

"YOU WILL CALL ME MASTER!!" the creature bellowed. "You will call me as you have been trained to do before I tear your body apart, traitor!"

Marcus stood his ground. "Vladimir, this church belonged to my friend, a man named Arthur Murray. This is his church. This is OUR church. You are not welcome here."

Not being anywhere near what would be considered human, Vladimir could not comprehend what he was experiencing at that moment. Watching his pupil grieve for food, not being called master and now being told... ORDERED... to leave a holy house. Never had the elder been subjected to this type of disrespect. He had only ever been used to having his words heeded immediately. Now this former human DARED to speak to him as if he were some type of equal?

It was far more than Vladimir was willing to bear; he ached with the barely contained desire to brutally decimate everyone in the church. But instead he held back, his bloodlust eclipsed only by his curiosity. He had to know... he *HAD* to know... why his pupil left. He stepped forward to face Marcus, glowering as he did so.

"I gifted you with powers no other vampire possessed. Among all your brethren, it was you whom I choose to rule by my side. You whom I choose to implement my plan to spread our clan to the outside world. I was to RULE this planet, to enslave the food and keep them under control, to bring forth a vampire awakening, and you were to assist in this conquest. You will tell me why you betrayed me."

The elder's words brought shock to the other vampires. World conquest? Marcus to rule with him? They knew nothing of this plan, they knew nothing of the role Marcus was supposed to play. When he first approached them with the idea of not returning to the clan, he only spoke of finding salvation. He never mentioned that Vladimir had tagged him as his right –hand man for world domination.

Thus did the vampires finally know the hidden truth; **Marcus walked away from power.** He walked away from a position where he would help rule over everyone and everything, and he did it to save himself and to save them, for a chance at a redemption that was not even promised but simply believed. Of all of them, Marcus had made the greatest sacrifice of all.

That truth had now galvanized the group. Fear and hopelessness, which reigned over them mere seconds before, were now replaced by a steely resolve to fight to the end. They would stand with Marcus no matter what the cost.

"Betray you? I guess you can call it that. We prefer to call it salvation. The real truth is I wanted to save the souls of myself and my friends. I was tired of killing people. Tired of hearing the screams and seeing the fear in the eyes of those I hunted. And my friends were tired of it as well. You would've never let us go, so we left. When you commanded us to go to Paris, you gave us the perfect opportunity to slip out. That bit of information has got to bother you, I imagine."

The demon visibly bristled at what he was hearing. Marcus could sense his old master's anger, and he relished in this moment to finally tell the evil bastard what he had been waiting to say for over 200 years. He leaned toward Vladimir just a bit, to emphasize his words.

"You may have turned us into monsters, Vladimir, but you never took our humanity. We hid it, nurtured it, and held on to it despite every evil deed we were forced to commit. We will not allow ourselves to be defined by what you've done to us. You wanted your answer, old man? You got it."

Pausing for a moment, Marcus finished with a last

warning. "You're going to pay for killing my friend. Somehow, some way, we're going to kill you tonight."

A strange calm fell over the ancient demon. He smiled and replied, calmly and softly, to his former pupil.

"I invite you to try."

It was at this moment, literally, that all hell broke loose.

WAR

BOOOOM!!!

This was the noise that reverberated through the church, a result of the church floor exploding like an atomic bomb. The power of the blast knocked the group across the front wall of the church, with enough force to leave indentations

Strewn under a heavy wooden pew, Marcus struggled to gather his senses. An attack was expected, but the group failed to anticipate the floor exploding upward. His ears rang and light flashes sparkled his vision, but he had no time to allow his dead body to recover. Vladimir just gained the upper hand and would not waste it. Marcus knew he would press his advantage, and defeating him (if that was even possible) was going to be hard enough as it was.

Meanwhile the elder creature, completely confident of his upcoming victory, slowly floated over to where Marcus lay.

Now was the time to act. Marcus waited until Vladimir was directly above him. With all his strength, he forcefully shoved the heavy pew into the air, where it smashed directly into the floating monster. The violent force of the hit drove Vladimir to the opposite end of the church, smashing into the row of candles Father Murray had lit earlier, the pew landing on top of him.

The rush of adrenaline gave Marcus new life. He staggered to his feet, shaking his head to clear the fog from his mind. This small break would not last long. Turning around, he saw the others recovering from the initial attack. They were shocked and battered, but now standing.

OK good, they're still here, Marcus thought. *I don't know how we're going to kill him. We have to figure out...*

That thought was interrupted, as Vladimir tossed off the debris laying on him, and rose to standing. Calm and determined, the elder started walking towards the group. There was no favoritism in his quest. Whomever he encountered would die first.

Marcus faced the oncoming creature, and was ready to intercept him, when that decision was taken out of his hand. Stephen Amare Morris pushed Marcus to the side and ran at full speed towards Vladimir.

The sound of his comrades yelling at him to stop rang in his ears. With each running step he took, visions of his past human life flashed in his mind. Going fishing with dad. Helping his grandmother cook Thanksgiving dinner. Losing his virginity to Tamika McAllister in a bedroom during a party. The smiles of pride on his parents faces when he told them he was joining the Army. Other scattered memories coming all too fast, a jumbled mishmash of experiences.

Stephen knew he was going to die today. Fully, truly die. But he was going to die on his terms. He couldn't stop his transformation into a vampire, but he could damn sure write the final chapter in how he would leave this Earth.

There was also a concrete belief in Marcus' plan. Stephen had no doubt God would forgive him. He had no doubt he would see his friends (and his grandmother) again.

See you all on the other side. Thanks for making this possible, Marcus. Wish I could tell you how thankful I am, but I gotta kill this motherfucker first. Give Vickie a hug for me, brother.

It took less than two seconds for Stephen to reach within inches of Vladimir, but he would get no closer. The elder's long dead left arm stabbed the air between them, clutching Stephen's throat and bringing his momentum to a complete stop.

Slowly, Vladimir brought Stephen's face close to his own. He intended to make quick work of this worthless walking corpse, but not before he reveled in his fear…

…except there was no fear in Stephen. Only determination. He couldn't speak, not with Vladimir's hand crushing his throat, but that was fine. The grenade he held in his hand would do all the talking.

Placing the grenade directly between him and his former master, Stephen closed his eyes, and pulled the pin.

Vladimir had just enough time to notice the round metal ball before it exploded.

A massive burst of black smoke and white fire erupted with an ear-splitting bang, strewing body parts across the church's inner sanctum. For the second time in three minutes, Vladimir had been violently knocked to the floor, driven into the mass of broken pews and floor boards piled against the back wall.

Pain was not usually something a vampire felt. Mostly it would be akin to an amputee having residual feelings where their limb used to be. But bloodsuckers *were* capable of feeling pain under certain circumstances. Thus while collecting his senses, did Vladimir discover he was minus most of his left arm. Where his hand and forearm had previously been, was now a burnt splintered stub. Blackened bits of skin hung off the remaining limb, covered in the black goo of vampire blood. Patches of dead muscle covered the exposed bone. He could feel burn marks on his face as well.

Laying in a crumpled heap upon the church wreckage, Vladimir could not help but feel a twinge of appreciation. The traitor had tricked him completely. Clever move, he thought.

Despite the loss of limb, Vladimir remained "alive", so to speak. The same could not be said of Stephen. Mutilated sections of the fallen soldier lay scattered across the area. The most intact piece, his head and upper body, landed not far from where the group stood. Still smoking from the blast.

"No!" Alexander screamed.

Shocked and saddened, Marcus could only look at the remains of his friend. He was all ready to take on Vladimir himself, to give the others a chance to attack and hopefully overwhelm him. Stephen made that sacrifice instead. But it was not in vain.

Mourning Stephen's loss, Marcus nonetheless kept his focus on the new current reality; Vladimir was severely injured. The suicide attack evened the odds. If there was ever a time to strike and press their attack, it was now.

"He's hurt," Marcus yelled back to his two remaining comrades. "We have to take him now!"

Those words were music to Alexander's ears. "What's your plan?"

"Hit him hard and fast. Let's see if we can rip him apart."

Gennady's face contorted into a wicked snarl. The muscles in his arms and back tensed up tight. For too long, he had waited. For too long, he had been the model of patience and calm. Even when killing his victims, he was always quick and clean about it. Simple puncture wounds on the neck were all the damage he would do. Excessive violence was not his style; he simply felt that type of carnage wasn't needed.

But it would be needed tonight.

Gennady had wanted this moment for centuries, and here it was. Rip apart Vladimir? He was all too happy to oblige. "With pleasure."

***

Wow. Still here, in the void, all by myself.

At least I was able to talk to Vicki. Didn't know if she'd be able to hear me but she did. The look on her face said so, haha.

I can't see what's going on in the church! I keep trying to reach out, but I can't see anything. Probably getting

blocked by that old asshole. Wish I could see his face when…
…who is that?
Someone's here! Kinda foggy, can't see who it is. Hey! Can you see me? I'm waving at you!
OMG...STEPHEN!!
OMG OMG OMG OMG!!!!
Gimme a hug! I'm so glad you're here! I didn't know if I was ever gonna see anyone again.
Wait wait... you did what?

LOSS

All he needed was a second.

One second was all Vladimir would require to unleash his powers on the traitors. To focus his energy, to direct his fury. To guarantee their death and his continued existence. Just one second. But the vampires refused to give him that second.

Marcus, Gennady and Alexander jumped on Vladimir just moments before, and their attack was relentless. Punching, kicking, tearing, like a pack of wolves fighting over a kill. The elder would attempt to rise and fight but would be brought down over and over. They had managed to pin him to a small space in the pile of broken concrete and wood.

The surprise grenade explosion had weakened him more then he thought. Vladimir has not counted on such a device, nor that his enemies would employ such unconventional tactics. He had made a... mistake? Impossible! He was a monster, a creation of the holy father Satan himself. Mistakes were for the food, not him. At most, there was a tactical miscalculation.

Suddenly, pair of hands grabbed Vladimir's head, and began trying to lift him...no, this was not that. Two other pairs of hands also grabbed Vladimir's head. They were not trying to lift Vladimir up; they were trying to rip his head from his body.

"I got him!" shouted Alexander. "Everybody grab on.

Pull, PULL!!"

It was almost over now. Alexander had positioned himself opposite Marcus and Gennady, with all three standing above Vladimir. He caught the bastard scurrying to hide further under the debris. Moving quickly, he reached down and clasped his hands around his former master's head, and began to pull with all his strength. This would have to be enough to finally kill him. Perhaps vampires COULD kill an elder after all.

The others jumped in and grabbed Vladimir's head as well. Gripping whatever part they could hold on, the vampires pulled with all their might. Muscles strained in Vladimir's neck, fighting against the grasp. But it would not be enough. Soon they would remove the head from its body. All they needed was a few more seconds.

All Vladimir needed was one.

The elder thrust his lone remaining hand towards the giant hole in the floor, his hand reaching out to the void. This was a call, and instantly the call was heard.

Like a tidal wave, a sea of thousands of large sewer rats exploded out of the hole. A sound of high pitched screeching had filled the room, as the vermin burst upon the vampires without warning, a hungry, violent swarming collective.

With his head free (and still attached), Vladimir rose to his feet. He could see the three vampires, no longer working close as a team but now random individuals fighting off being eaten, flailing about as they tried to get the rats off them. The vicious rodents would surely devour them in due time, but all Vladimir wanted from them was a distraction. Now he could pick off the lying traitors one by one, starting with the vampire closest to him; Gennady.

His body covered by the rat swarm, Gennady desperately fought to get them off. Grabbing and flinging them off his body, as many as he could. The vermin were attacking him at every angle, even going after his eyes to try to blind him. Therefore, he would not see his doom right in front of him.

Vladimir stepped to within mere feet of Gennady's flailing body. "направи пут," he spoke, and suddenly the rats moved to create a clear space on Gennady's chest...a clear path to his death.

Vladimir growled, reared back his good hand, and tore it directly into Gennady's chest, straight through his spine and all the way out the back. Just as quickly, he pulled the hand back, clutching Gennady's heart in his hands. A scream roared from the native Russian's mouth.

What happened next took just several seconds, but to Gennady felt like forever. The life force which had sustained him, which made him kill humans to feast on their blood, was escaping him at a rapid pace. The rats fell off his body, their work done. On the brink of collapse, Gennady locked eyes with Vladimir. He tried to say something, a last act of defiance... but then came the brightness.

A large shining ball of white light appeared in front of him. Was anybody else seeing this, he thought. Then he saw them...Stephen and Mila. They were in the light! He saw them, and they saw him. Mila was saying something Gennady could not hear, she was waving at him, motioning for him to come to them. And so he did.

As he walked closer to the light, he instantly felt better. He could walk fast and strong, as he always had done. The hole in his chest was healed, and he could...he could feel a heartbeat! He was alive! Then was Gennady completely in the light. Stephen and Mila ran up to him and hugged him tight. This was real, he could feel them, he could hold and touch them. Overwhelmed with happiness, Gennady shed a tear, and smiled.

What Vladimir saw was the vampire teeter back and forth, his eyes looking off into the distance. Concentrating on something else, something Vladimir could not see. Finally, the vampire named Gennady smiled... *SMILED?!...* and collapsed.

Too many things were happening tonight the elder had

never experienced or seen before. Why would the traitor smile before his death? Part of the anticipation for tonight for Vladimir was not only killing them, but reveling in their pain and fear. Taking immense pleasure in denying them their quest. Yet this vampire died smiling, looking like a happy fool. He simply denied giving Vladimir that little bit of pleasure.

The elder's face contorted into a sneer of anger. This night had already cost him far more than he thought it would. Losing the arm was bad enough (he was certain the Holy Father would grant him a new one) but now he was even being denied the pleasure of the kill. It was more than the monster could stand. Vladimir was ready to put an end to this, to finish this fiasco, and if it meant not getting the enjoyment he wanted then so be it. He would get his jollies by torturing some humans on the way back home.

However, that would have to wait. There was work to do. There was still punishment to be given.

The rats summoned by Vladimir had already retreated back down into the gaping crater in the church floor, leaving their last two victims barely mobile. Alexander lay on the floor near the pit, gasping for air. Marcus lay slumped against the front door of the church. Both bore the new wounds of their recent attack. Tassels of ripped flesh hung from multiples places on their bodies, deep cuts where chunks of flesh were bitten off, streaks of leaking black blood where the cuts ran deepest.

The vampires clung to consciousness by a string, but they could not afford a moment's rest. Every second they wasted was a second closer for Vladimir. Indeed, the elder was almost upon them.

Alexander knew this and counted the seconds. Laid out on his back on the floor, he saw the demon walk closer and closer to him.

I bet he's pissed off now. Real pissed. How'd it feel losing that arm, Vlady? Bet you didn't see that coming. My man Stephen set you up real good. Here's where I finish what he started, asshole.

With a sudden burst of lightning speed, Alexander shot up from his prone position. With his left hand he grabbed Vladimir's shoulder, and with his right hand, shoved a long sharp piece of wood right into Vladimir's chest, dead center where his heart would be. It was a perfect strike, and had Alexander been human, it would have been a complete kill shot.

Alas, Alexander stopped being human 200 years ago. He was now a vampire, and while his attack was a textbook example of how to kill a bloodsucker, it only works when a living human does it. Alexander was no human, and Vladimir was no mere vampire.

After a night time of one disappointment after another, Vladimir finally smiled. The wooden stake imbedded in his chest crumpled apart in dusty pieces, falling onto the ground. Skin and dead muscle closed over the hole in Vladimir's chest.

The elder grinned at Alexander, their faces separated by mere inches. The grin got bigger, until Vladimir finally laughed.

Alexander was usually the funny guy, the one who cracked jokes, the one who found humor in pretty much anything. He found no humor in Vladimir's cackle. No trace of happiness or merriment or glee. It was the sound of a thousand demons loudly laughing deep from the pits of hell. The sound that foretold of bad things about to happen, and Alexander knew who the recipient of those things were.

Hey God, it's me. I really hope you're real. I really hope Marcus was right about you. Help him out, ya dig? He's gonna need it.

Vladimir quickly clasped his hands to Alexander's head, an ironic reversal of their position just minutes earlier. This time though, the elder succeeded where Alexander did not.

A violent jerk upward, and Alexander's head tore apart from his body. The rest of Alexander shook awkwardly, before crumpling to the ground in a lifeless heap.

His victory over the traitor complete, Vladimir didn't

even bother looking at Alexander's face; closed eyes, gritting teeth, a realization that his time was done.

Instead the elder pitched the vampire's head behind him, as if disposing of some garbage. After all, his night was not yet done. One last task before he returned home. One last vampire to kill.

Marcus.

THE LAST

It all came down to this.

Marcus pulled himself off from the ground. Standing directly across from him several yards away was Vladimir. The final battle between pure evil and accidental evil was set to begin.

Really, there was no other way this was going to happen. Marcus wished for a different outcome. He worked for it, sacrificed for it, paid for it in years and years of planning. Marcus and the others trekked across the Atlantic Ocean, to not just a different country but a different hemisphere, just to put enough distance between themselves and their enslaver. Surely even Vladimir's telepathic powers could not stretch across the ocean. Yet find them he did. All their planning, all for naught. Vladimir found them regardless.

I can't say I'm surprised. So many other things had gone our way for so long. It was bound to go the other way sooner or later.

Maybe this is how it was meant to finish. God is testing me, aren't you Lord? I think THIS is the time to use the toys Satan gave me.

And maybe God, just this once, is OK with it.

Vladimir stood his ground, his eyes locked on Marcus yet not moving a muscle. He had underestimated the group already and paid for that mistake with most of his left arm. While he did not fear Marcus, Vladimir remained cautious nonetheless. No telling what the liar had up his sleeve.

Despite his caution, he would find out soon enough.

"Tell me, Marcus. Are you satisfied? Look around you. Is this what you risked damnation for? Was this worth your betrayal of me? Everything and everyone you hold dear is gone. Your fellow traitors lay wasted. Your human female has left you. Your priest feeds the maggots. You have failed."

Flashing a grin, Marcus said "I got to see you lose an arm. Not a total loss." That was a funny quip, Marcus thought. Alexander would be proud.

"Those will be your last wo -"

Without warning, Marcus screamed. Out of nowhere, flames engulfed Vladimir's entire body. Every inch of him covered in hellfire.

This was a little trick Vladimir had shown him many years prior. One of several powers granted him. But Marcus had not used the fire since that time and wondered if he would remember how.

There was no screaming from Vladimir. Instead, he tensed his body, balled up his fists, and began to mutter words older than humanity itself. His body was tense and rigid, fully braced for the winds to come. Dust and paper began to float around him, then darting in a circular motion, riding the powerful air bursts gaining in intensity.

Where Vladimir stood in flames, there were now mighty gusts of wind swirling about him. As if a small hurricane entered the church. The flames stood no chance. Seconds later, every trace of fire had vanished, followed by the fading wind. Only Vladimir remained.

Marcus had managed to surprise Vladimir, and turned his alabaster skin to charcoal grey, but had done nothing more. The elder still survived, shifting his gaze to Marcus.

There was nothing left to say. Words would not matter now. Moving faster than his normal pace, Vladimir began his march toward his former pupil.

Marcus knew he would not surrender, but what was his next step? He could not summon the other powers

Vladimir had given him. Too many years, too much hostility towards his condition to even practice his gifts. There was only flying, the one gift he would nurture and engage in. And he would not under any means fly away. Which meant physical combat.

Well, that was fine with him.

Taking his own steps, Marcus moved toward his former master. As he moved closer, his pace quickened, as it did for Vladimir.

In an instant, the battle had begun.

***

How many minutes had passed?

How much time had elapsed?

How much hatred could two individuals harbor for one another?

In this case, it would seem endless.

Moments earlier, the vampire and demon slammed into each other with a ferocity unmatched in recent times. Hard enough to crack bones. Both combatants rained blows on the other. Each trying something, anything to gain the upper hand.

For Marcus, this was nothing short of survival, with a heavy dose of vengeance sprinkled in. 200 years of pent up frustration and anger were being unleashed now. Every punch he landed, every wound he would slice open, every scream he uttered, carried some of that anger with it. Whatever the outcome, Marcus knew that he would at least purge himself of all of it.

For Vladimir, this was also about survival. How would it look to the Dark Father, a failure of this magnitude? How would he still command the respect and fear of the vampire clan back in Sarajevo? It was true one vampire could not kill an elder. Hundreds of vampires? There was no clear cut answer for that question, and the result might be a different story. Vladimir learned the hard way tonight, that even HE had his limits.

And so, it came to be, in this church on this night, two mortal enemies clashed in a battle for their very existence.

Marcus had engaged Vladimir in close quarters combat. Figuring the elder would not be free to use the full extent of his powers if the fight was directly upon him, and for a while he was right. He had gotten right into Vladimir's chest, grabbing him in a tight bear hug to restrict his movement. Baring his fangs, the vampire sank his teeth into Vladimir's neck and reared his head back, tearing off a chunk of flesh.

That should have slowed down the demon, giving Marcus time to inflict more damage. Instead, Vladimir plunged his long sharp fingernails into Marcus' chest. In one motion, he swung around and sent Marcus flying, smacking hard into the back wall of the church with enough force to embed his body two feet deep.

Stunned by the impact, Marcus tried to gather his senses and prepare the next attack, but he was too late. Above him, a small black cloud formed within seconds, and from this cloud a bolt of lightning shot forth and struck Marcus. The blast blew him off the wall, this time right to the floor, landing face first with a hard thud. Two heartbeats later, a second bolt struck Marcus in the back. His screams reverberated throughout the church.

Finally, for good measure, a third bolt struck him. This blast flipped him in the air, and he landed lifelessly, a wounded mass of a burnt bruised body.

The relentless onslaught was exacting a heavy toll from Marcus. Lifting his arms was almost impossible; they felt like heavy bags of sand. Severe burns covered his torso from front to back.

This was, of course, all Vladimir's doing. From his vantage point, he motioned his hands like a maestro from hell, and the lightning was his symphony. It had been a long time since Vladimir used this particular skill set, and he found it to be quite enjoyable. Especially since he personally gifted

Marcus with this power, and the knowledge needed to maintain control. Had he forgotten how to wield it?

Drifting in and out of focus, Marcus alternated between finding a different plan of attack, and cursing himself for not being better prepared. The latter could be debated, the former was almost a moot point.

Where the body was wrecked and damaged, the will was strong and defiant. Marcus summoned what strength he had left, and slowly began pushing himself up from the floor. He then felt a sudden jerk upward, only to be forcefully thrown back to the ground. Again, pulled up and slammed down, then again. Marcus was nothing more than a plaything now, much like a cat toying with a dead bird.

Marcus laid on his back, facing upward toward the ceiling. A dark figure appeared above him. Marcus had no choice but to face his former master. He did not even have the strength to look away. The vampire wanted to fight back, but there was nothing left to give. The wall and the lightning were too much for even his iron will to overcome, and the slamming was simply the icing on the cake. He would bear witness to his own demise.

Exactly how Vladimir wanted it.

The demon stood over Marcus' prone body. He could sense how weak his ex-pupil was, yet still he struggled to move, to fight back somehow. All he could manage was lifting his head an inch from the ground and exhaling in short grunts.

"And this is how it ends, Marcus. Your betrayal has cost me more than you can imagine, however I will use your death and the end of your fellow traitors as a warning to other vampires who would dare to consider leaving. Even at the moment of your destruction, you will still serve me."

That comment would have made a fully conscious Marcus sick to his stomach, but at this moment it barely registered. There was no stopping what Vladimir was about to do.

As he struggled to stay aware and awake, his thoughts turned to his friends, the ones who trusted him and believed in his quest. Their salvation was still a possibility. It was possible that he had done just enough to get them to their redemption. They got to walk into a church and not turn to ash. So maybe he DID succeed after all. He could still dream of Heaven, could he not? The elder could not take that away from him. He could not take away *hope*.

His thoughts then turned to Vicki, the woman who captured his heart. The last thing he expected on this journey was to fall in love, and yet it happened. A beautiful woman with the world at her feet fell in love with him. She loved him and valued him and accepted him for everything he was. This truly was what gave Marcus the belief that God could still save them. She was away from here and safe, at least Marcus hoped.

You won't get her, you bastard. She's gone. She HAS to be. She'll live to a ripe old age while you sulk in your cave…

"Your bitch will die tonight," Vladimir scowled. "I will scour the city for her, I will find your scent, it will lead me to her, and I will turn her in the same manner I turned you. She will serve as the devil's whore, and she will curse you forever for her plight."

No. NO NO NO NOOO! Please God, please protect her. Take my soul, take anything, please don't…don't…let him take her…

The final act of defiance from Marcus, was his refusal to lose hope. He would die here believing that Vicki would be safe. He would not give into panic, to despair, or even the likely reality of Vladimir's words.

He would hold on to love. He would hold on to hope.

For Vladimir, this moment had at last arrived. The wait had been long enough. Now the acolyte of Satan would claim his prize.

Vladimir raised his right arm…
…started a mighty swing…
…and froze.

Vladimir heard the sound before he felt it. He didn't quite register what the noise was, only that his body was unable to move through no control of his own. His right arm stayed stuck in mid swing, the intended target Marcus still laying beneath him. Try as he might, Vladimir could not move his arm, nor any other body part.

Then he looked down, his eyes the only part that could move, and just like that he knew the why of his condition. A long, jagged piece of wood stuck out from his chest, dripping his own blood down to the point.

He heard a second noise; a loud grunt, and felt the stake shoved further through his body. The elder eked out a small gasp; for the first time in his undead life, he felt PAIN.

From the corner of his eye, he could make out a figure coming around from behind him on his right side. Finally stopping in front of him, to make sure he knew who had done this.

For the second time this night, Vladimir had been staked. But this time was much different. This was not a vampire staking him. The hand that guided this instrument belonged to a human, and she had a name.

Vicki Ramos.

She would be the last thing Vladimir would ever see.

The dissolution of the elder happened quite fast. Death shudders rattled the demon's body. Muscles and skin, already taut and weathered from centuries of unnatural life, receded into nothing. The expression on the demon's face told a simple story of realization; he had just been destroyed by a human.

Vladimir...the mighty elder demon vampire, soon to be the right hand of Satan himself...crumbled to the floor of a church like a dusty bag of bones, arms and legs falling off like withered tree limbs. A low hiss escaped the disintegrated husk as it continued to deteriorate after the fall.

Finally it was over.

GOOD-BYE

Vicki thought she was too late.

Though in reality the battle in the church did not last hours, it felt that way to Vicki. She scrambled around the outside part of the entire church, desperate to find some way back inside. The front doors would not open, a side door would not open, even some basement windows in the back would not shatter no matter how hard Vicki kicked.

There also an eerie quiet outside. Vicki imagined there would be loud noises and smashing and maybe screaming, but she heard nothing. She pressed her ear against a side door and could hear muffled sounds, and this was the only way for her to hear anything. To her, it sounded like a TV with the volume turned down real low.

It made no sense to her, but then again nothing about any of this made sense. She was in love with a real live vampire, and he and his friends were fighting some monster super vampire inside a church. Normal had long since left the building.

Vicki guessed (correctly, it turned out) that Vladimir must be using some kind of magic to keep everything quiet. Perhaps to avoid dealing with the cops or any other distractions? Made sense to her.

Suddenly, she a felt powerful vibration, and she could hear a sound of a window breaking. Running around to the back of the church, she indeed found one of the windows busted open. Crouching down to peek in, she saw a large empty space underneath the church where the floor should have been. She could see some parts of the inside, and saw small flashes of movement.

And so it was that Vicki crawled into the small window space, made her way through the rubble and into the church, hid well enough to not be seen, grabbed a long broken piece of wood, snuck up behind Vladimir, and drove it through his back with everything she had. Then pushed it in even deeper for good measure.

Vicki wasn't quite sure what gave her the fortitude to face the monster and look into his eyes. Love, perhaps? Anger? Probably both. Whatever it was, she made sure the demon saw exactly who it was that killed him. She wanted him to know he failed, and she wanted him to know SHE did it.

Now the deed was done, and whatever had remained of Vladimir crumbled into piles of dust. Her full attention turned to Marcus, and she gasped at what she saw. There were burns on his entire torso, pools of blood under him, cuts and bruises and open wounds from his face on down.

Vicki's heart dropped. Kneeling down beside him, she gently caressed his face, and cleaned the dust from his eyes. Her own tears started to fall, landing on Marcus' face before rolling down his cheek. This seemed to wake him, and he stirred with a groan.

"Baby, it's me. I'm here," Vicki whispered to her love. "It's over. Marcus, it's over. Vladimir is dead."

Marcus' eyelids fluttered, then opened. He then smiled, a genuine smile of happiness. "I saw. Saw everything." He winced from one of the numerous bouts of pain in his body, paused a few seconds to let it pass, and then continued.

"You did it, Vicki. I'm so damn *proud* of you. Heh. You know, when I told you about only a human killing an elder, that wasn't an invitation." He closed his eyes and laughed a little.

Vicki managed a smile as well. "I wanna hug you so

bad right now. But we got to go. Who knows if the cops will show up, and Mila's outside."

The woman who committed one miracle tonight was seeking to make another.

I am saving this man. Do you hear me, Lord? I am walking out of here with him, and I'm taking him home and he's never gonna hurt again.

Marcus reached up to caress her face, catching tears on his fingers. Words could not express how much he wanted to stay. How he wished he could dry her tears and see her smile every day. Life in this new century with his new love, what an adventure it would have been.

"I love you, Vicki." Marcus fought back the increasing difficulty of talking and breathing. "Thank you. For everything."

"Shhh shh, stop it. Don't talk, babe. I'm gonna carry you if I have to but we are going home." The last few words were spoken through choked back sobs.

"For showing me how to love again," Marcus spoke. "For giving me the hope we needed. For being who you are."

"I love you, Lady Ramos. And I... I al... ways..."

Vicki could not see it, but Marcus could. A ball of white light, settling just above Marcus. It started small, but increased in size as it came closer to him. There was a peace in the light. Marcus could feel the warmth of the glow bathe over him, and as it did his pain lessened, his scars healed, his breathing stabilized.

He stared further into the light. The hard bright glare at the center softened, and...was that Mila? And the others! Alexander, Stephen, Gennady...and Father Murray! He saw them all together. Looking healthy and whole. They were waving at him, trying to get his attention. Did he hear something? Their voices...he could hear them! Mila was motioning for him to join them, and her voice rang clear in his mind.

It's OK, Marcus. You did it. Your plan worked. We're saved! OMG you were right, you were right!! We're all going to Heaven.

Let's go, boss. They're ready for us. Tell Vicki I'll see her when she gets here!

Vicki could not see the light, but she knew something was happening. She could see it in his face. He seemed calm, and moved without effort, without straining from the pain. He looked past her, somewhere above and behind her. He looked...ready.

That's when she knew. Marcus's plan had worked. He would be going to Heaven. But this also meant he would not be going home with her.

Vicki began to cry, heaving sobs and tears. Tears of happiness, that Marcus and the others had found salvation. Tears of sorrow, because the price for that salvation was the end of his time on Earth.

Marcus leaned forward, and gently kissed Vicki on her lips. For several seconds, he held that pose. To savor one last touch, to let her know just how much he had loved her.

"Mila says hi," he said, and Vicki laughed between the sobs. "Go live your life, Vicki. Chase your dreams, conquer the world. I'll be watching."

Vicki looked at him, staring one last time into his eyes. "I love you, Marcus. I always will."

The light beckoned. Marcus' spirit, long held captive in his vessel of skin and bone, stepped free into the light. The others rushed him and hugged him tight. Their dream was achieved. They made it.

His body slumped against Vicki. She could feel something leave him then.

It was over. He was gone.

The finality hit Vicki hard. She held him close to her, and screamed. A wail of grief and despair, of love and loss. For a long time, she cried immensely and deeply. For a long time, she gently rocked him back and forth, telling him she would never forget him, telling him how proud SHE was of him.

I know you had to go. God, I'm gonna miss you. But

you did it, Marcus. You're not the only one who's proud.
 Go find your wife. I bet she's there, and to be honest she had you first. Just keep our one night a secret.
 I love you, Marcus. Forever and a day.

EPILOGUE

The boxes stood in the corner of a bedroom stacked like mini cardboard towers, and Vicki Ramos couldn't figure out which one to tackle first. Should she worry about hanging up the clothes? Maybe put up the knick knacks on the bookshelf? Put the shoes in the closet first before anything? She did not quite know at the moment.

What she did know was that Warren better hurry his ass up here.

"Husband!" she cried out. "Your wife needs your help."

It was not long before Warren Patrick came bounding up the stairs. "What's up? You OK? The baby OK?"

Vicki rubbed her large pregnant belly, then leaned against her hubby's chest. "We're OK, daddy. But I need one of those boxes brought down, and I'm not doing it. Too busy carrying your child here."

Warren placed his arms around his pregnant bride. "See, that's all you call me for. Favors and moving boxes. Not even gonna ask me..."

"Fuck outta here with that!" Vicki said jokingly. "You got me married and pregnant, you can stop using those lines now. Slacker."

Within minutes, the top box Warren had brought down was open and getting emptied. Vicki had a lot of work to do putting up all of her personal stuff from her old apartment. She would be living in a house now, and the extra space meant she had to decorate differently. Warren was downstairs dealing with the heavy stuff, and setting up his man cave, which gave Vicki alone time to set up her stuff however she wanted. It took close to 5 minutes of rummaging through her things, when she came across an item that made her pause.

An album by Earth, Wind & Fire.

Emotions overcame her. Being pregnant made her even more emotional than she normally was. All her old feelings and memories came flooding back.

It had been almost three years since the night at the church. To Vicki it still felt like yesterday. She held Marcus till almost dawn. Held him while his body slowly turned to dust and disappeared. Finally able to gather herself, she left before the sun rose, sneaking out through the side door and making the lonely trip back home.

The events had shaken Vicki to her core. For days she slept in at her parent's house (she could not bear to sleep alone), taking comfort in their company and crying while her father held her. She told her parents she had gone through a painful break up, which technically was true. It took weeks for her to come around feeling normal, and to get back into the groove of work and life.

During this whole time, Warren and she had grown close. He would come by to see her without her asking, bringing flowers and words of support, and hugs whenever she needed them. Vicki was putting herself back together, and while she grieved for the loss of a loved one, she was also ready to love again, and did not even realize it until they had gone on their third date. His feelings for her were genuine and real, and while watching him tell a funny story about his childhood over a picnic in Central Park, she realized she grown to care for him quite deeply. Warren too, had fallen hard for her. True, he always wanted to date her, but this was beyond dating or a crush. This was real love, and they both came to that same place.

In the time since, love turned to engagement, then to marriage, then to pregnancy. To where she was right now, standing in the master bedroom of the house in Staten Island her and Warren recently purchased. Coming across a reminder of the vampire she loved.

She still remembered him. She remembered her night in the hallway chatting with Mila, and how she gave her life to save hers. She remembered her and Marcus talking on the roof. Vicki was happy now, sincerely happy, but she never forgot Marcus.

She cried a little, and hoped they were OK. Vicki thought that maybe Marcus would try to contact her, maybe send her signs. But there had been nothing.

Several minutes passed while Vicki went to the bathroom to wipe away her tears. She stayed in there trying to figure out where to hang some pictures, when she was startled by a song she hadn't heard since a certain night.

THAT'S THE WAY OF THE WORLD was playing in her room.

She hurried back to her room to find the album had somehow made it from the floor on to the record player by the window. Somehow the phonograph had turned on and was playing this particular song.

Was Warren playing a trick on her? She peeked out the window and saw him outside messing with the outdoor patio set. There was no way he could have done this and made it back downstairs in time. Besides, while Warren loved music and had a deep knowledge of various acts and songs, he couldn't have known the significance of this track to her. Vicki had never shared the details of that night with anyone. So who…?

It's about time, Marcus. I was thinking you forgot about me.

How do you like the house? I know, it's a lot bigger than my apartment. You can stay and check it out, just don't go scaring Warren, alright? He's good to me, and he's gonna be a good daddy.

Yeah, I know, me having a kid. I never thought I would be the mommy type, but real talk, having a baby growing in your belly makes you change your mind. I'm so in love already, and I'm not gonna know if it's a girl or boy until I give birth. Going real old school here!

Thank you for contacting me. This puts my mind at ease. I know you're OK now. I know you made it. I knew you would.

Take care, Marcus. Love you.

Vicki walked out the room. To walk downstairs and be with her husband, to continue her journey, to chase her dreams as Marcus told her.

To live her life.

The record player stopped, and a peaceful silence remained.